D1373167

Thuggin' at the Altar

By: Denora Boone & Jenica Johnson

AUG 1 6

Copyright 2015 by Denora Boone and Jenica
Johnson

Published by Anointed Inspirations Publications

Denora's Thank You's

I'll keep this short and sweet cause some of yall may not even read this…lol but I thank God for this wonderful opportunity to be a blessing to His people through writing. No one understands how hard it is to write a book let alone a Christian one. But the end results make it all worth it.

Thank you to my husband Byron and our children Jalen, Elijah, Mekiyah, and Isaiah for supporting me and putting up with the long nights of writing. I do this for you.

Thank you to Jenica and Charles Johnson for hopping on this ride with us. The two of you are a pure blessing and I pray that you receive everything that God has in store for you. You are a blessing not only to AIP but to my family as well. Yall are truly our family…even if Charles be trying it as a manager!!!

To our readers, thank you for not only continuing to love and support us but by believing in and accepting what it is we do!

Love, Dee

Follow me

Twitter: @mzboone27

Instagram: @mzboone81

Facebook: Author Denora Boone

Jenica's Thank You's

I thank God for my gift of storytelling. For as long as I can remember I've always had a journal and a book. I didn't understand it then but I fully understand it now. If I don't change but one life, that's all that matters to me.

To my husband, Charles Johnson you mean so much to me. You are behind the scenes pushing Denora and I to do our best. You praise us and you critic us and for that I'm grateful. My kids Nozi, Arianna and CJ mommy love yall with all my being. I know I stay super busy, but I'm never too busy to stop what I'm doing to support what yall doing.

Denora I've thoroughly enjoyed writing this book with you. If the readers really knew this was off the cuff, around the dinner table talk and boom here's the book. I know we have plenty of work to do and this is only the beginning for AIP.

My readers I love you guys dearly. When I want to give up, God sends one of you to encourage me. I pray that yall enjoy what Denora and I have put together for you all.

Love, Jenica

Follow me:

Twitter: AuthorJenica

Facebook: Author Jenica

Facebook Reading Group:
fearfully_wonderfully_me

Instagram: @fearfully_wonderfully_me

Gavon

It was a little past midnight when me and Po Cat ran up on a lick. We sat back and watched as he took the big duffle bag that was filled with money out his trunk. I was breathing hard and it was cold. The white smoke was the only thing that can be seen coming from my mouth as I tightened my hoodie around my face. As Po Cat handed me the gun, pictures of my grandmothers face popped up, I could even hear her voice so clearly, *Gavon you gone die or go to jail in them streets*. If she only knew I was doing this for her. I hated to see my grandmother struggle to take care of us. She lived in the same house for over forty years, slap in the middle of the hood. All I ever wanted was to get her out and move her somewhere peaceful.

"Gee! Take the shot man, we got a lot riding on this," my partner knocked me out of my day dream.

I gripped the gun loosely and cocked it, this would be my first time using a gun I never even held one. I aimed it at old dude and was scared to squeeze the trigger. Before I could build up the courage to pull the trigger of my .38 special, I heard two shots go off and I dropped the gun I was holding too see that my partner in crime was holding a smoking gun staring at me through bloodshot eyes with a menacing mug.

"Come on Gee, I knew you wasn't about this life. Just stick to the drug game lil Gee," he said as we got up to run up to our victim. He grabbed the bag and ran off into the night. When we made it back to the trap house and empty the contents on the dining room table. Our eyes got big as saucers when all the cash fell out the bag. After counting it, it equaled up to about 50 g's.

"Alright Gee here's your cut," Po Cat said. I looked at the little measly five thousand dollars and pushed it back towards him.

"Nah bruh, I deserve way more than that right there," I pointed at the money.

"What makes you think that play boy? You ain't do nothing but show up."

I snatched the five g's and left him sitting at the table. It was already late and I knew my grandmother was up roaming around the house wondering where I was. Tomorrow was Sunday and she probably already had her clothes out for church. I accompanied my grandmother to church every Sunday morning and nothing was going to change that tonight. My plan was to put the money up in a shoe box and continue to save until I could get out the hood. I walked about two blocks until I made it home. The porch light was on and the small little lamp in the living room by my grandmothers reading chair was on, so I knew she was up reading her Bible.

"Gavon is that you?"

"Yes ma'am," I eased the door shut.

"Get in here so I can see you."

I walked around the corner into the sitting area where she was sitting with her Bible in her lap.

My grandmother was a beautiful sight to see, I assumed she was around 70 years old but she would never tell me her age. She put you in the mind of Ruby Dee the actress. She had her grey hair braided back in two French braids that went past her shoulders, her reading glasses sat on the top of her nose and she had her old housecoat and slippers on.

"Where you been? I get on to you every day about coming in my house late. You would think I was wrong if I changed the locks. We got church in a few hours, gone on upstairs and rest them bloodshot eyes. And make sure you take a shower fo' you go to church. I don't want Rev. smelling that weed on you," my grandmother said before looking back down at her Bible.

Mama Jean didn't play any games with me, I knew she would cut me like a bad habit but the streets was where I desired to be. If only she knew my plan was to take us out the ghetto and move her into something new before she left this earth, then she would understand why I'm always in the streets. I walked up the squeaky stairs up to my room. My grandmother raised my mother and her siblings in this same house. It was an old white two story house, I slept in my mother's old room. I raised enough money to upgrade my bed, the springs were killing me with my old bed.

I kicked off my Jordan's and pulled my hoodie off. I didn't even bother to pull the cover back because by the time my eyes closed Mama Jean would be back up here beating my back trying to wake me up. I left so many things in this room just like my mother had it and I often wondered what it would be like with her here. It took me years to come to grips with my reality but without my grandmother I knew I wouldn't have been able to make it.

Buzz…buzz, the vibrations of my phone startled me out of my sleep. I pulled the phone out to see Chardonnay calling, blowing out hot air I answered.

"Talk to me," I said into the phone.

"Where you at? I came by the house and Mama Jean said you wasn't there, so where you been Gavon? Let me find out you been sneaking around. I told you don't play with a chick like me," she yapped into the phone. I had to pull my phone from my ear because she was talking so loud.

"Aye man listen, I'm home in my bed. I got church in the morning so I'll holla at you later," I hung up in her face. Chardonnay was ghetto fabulous and was half of the reason I couldn't keep money in my pocket. I had to keep her with the latest clothes, nails and bundles. It was all good because she made me look good and a lot of the streets dudes gave me respect because of her. I knew when she seen me she was going to slap me for hanging up but the sun was already creeping through the curtains and I had only got about two hours of sleep.

Mama Jean

"Lord this grandson of mine gone send me to my grave early," I said out loud as I struggled to get up the stairs. My knees were getting the best of me and my fibro myalgia was acting up this morning. Nothing was going to keep me from church this **today**, not even my hard headed grandson.

"Gavon…Gavon," I shook him violently. "Get up boy and get ready for church, breakfast almost ready too."

I climbed back down my twelve steps to check on my homemade biscuits that Gavon loved so much. I stirred the grits and dropped some cheese in them and a little milk to make them creamy. The bacon was sizzling in my black cast iron frying pan, most women didn't want to cook bacon on the stove because they were scared to get popped with the grease from the bacon. I guess that was the new generation women, I wanted all my stuff cooked the way I seen my mother cook it back in the day. I grabbed my greens out of the refrigerator and placed them on the stove and took the ham out and sat it on the counter. All I wanted to do once I got out of church was warm up the food and make some cornbread and rice.

After turning everything off and fixing Gavon's plate I went into my room and got dressed. I had Gavon move me downstairs so I could move around better. Gavon ran the streets but whatever I asked him to do he did. I knew him running the streets was coming to an end soon I just didn't want it to end with his life. I pulled my knee highs out of the plastic ball and slipped them on walking to my packed closet to pull out my favorite dress and my flats. I unbraided my plaits and placed some bobby pins in my hair.

"Mama Jean this good," Gavon said stuffing his mouth with bacon and biscuits at the same time.

"I forgot your honey. You know you can't eat them biscuits without honey."

"Mama Jean I'm just about finish now," he laughed.

We finished breakfast and headed out the door, Gavon wasn't too fond of my old school 1989 Crown Vic but it got me everywhere I needed to go. Pulling up at Greater Baptist, I slung my big car in my parking spot and got out. Gavon came around to help me and we walked in church together like we did every Sunday. The older he got the more afraid I was that he wasn't going to come home one Saturday night. All I do is walk around and pray until he hit the door.

"Mother Jean you looking good," First Lady kissed my cheek.

"Thank you beautiful."

"And how are you Gavon? You taking care of Mother?'

"As much as she would let me," they laughed.

"What's funny? I'm not too old to take care of myself," I retaliated.

Church was rocking today, I looked over at Gavon and even he was engaged as well. Rev. Rockmore called for the ones that wanted to give their lives over to Christ. I closed my eyes and said a silent prayer that Gavon would get up and walk to the altar. I longed for the day he would give his life to God. I opened my eyes slightly and peeked to the right where he was sitting and he hadn't moved. It was okay, I was gone keep on praying until God changed his heart.

———

"Slow down eating that food Gavon. Why you rushing," I eyed him as he stuffed the food down his throat.

"I got to go and see about Chardonnay."

"Oh Lord, what's wrong with your little girlfriend. Gavon I told you to be extra careful around her. I know her type and as long as you running the streets and spending all your money on her, she will be there. But if something happens to you, Lord forbid, she's gone."

"She wouldn't do that Mama Jean, you don't know her like that. I'm gone bring her around more so you guys can spend some time together."

"Nope see that's where you got me messed up at. I'm old but I ain't crazy, white wine, oops I meant Chardonnay look like she a klepto and I don't want none of my fine china going missing."

Seeing Gavon laugh at me put a smile on my face, "Mama Jean you are a mess. Let me wash these dishes before I go."

I walked in my room and changed into my housecoat and slippers before I got comfortable. I was gone sit and watch Lifetime movies all day. I went to inspect my kitchen before Gavon left for the day, he know I didn't play about my pots being greasy.

"Gavon, did you put a capful of bleach in your dish water when you wash them dishes," I yelled from the bottom of the stairs. He came running down with his baggy jeans and white shirt.

"Yes ma'am," he kissed me on my cheek. "Don't wait up on me, I'll make it home."

"Gavon stop saying that, every time you walk out the door I'm worried. I pray you make it home tonight."

"I will Mama Jean," he said over his shoulder.

Gavon

"Aye Chardonnay open the door," I hung up and slid my phone in my pocket. Chardonnay stayed in a little townhouse on the other side of the hood, it was like a baby projects. She answered the door with all those ugly rollers in her head. One thing I noticed was she had her makeup on, so I knew she was about to head out.

"Where you going on a Sunday? You did all that texting and whining about spending time with you and you about to leave."

"Yes I was about to leave because I thought your grandma was going to be selfish and keep you to herself today. You know that old woman don't like me."

"Watch your mouth when you talking about that one. You know what, go ahead and go where you were going. I can't stand being around you when you get in one of those moods, my grandmother has nothing to do with what we have. Yes, I'm gone go to church with her because she hardly ask for anything if you got a problem with that, then we may need to rethink this whole relationship thing."

"It ain't even like that Gee, I just know she don't care for me and I feel like she purposely does stuff."

"She ain't checking for you like that Chardonnay, trust me."

"Well since you here, you want to take me to the mall before they close."

"Here take this," I hand her a few hundred. "I don't do that shopping thing. I'll be back by the time you get back."

I headed to the block to see what was going on. I was still in my feelings about the measly 5g's my partner gave me last night. It was all good though because I was already plotting on my next lick and he was not gone be part of it.

"What's going on bruh," my little cousin dapped me up.

"Nothing bruh, what's going on up here today?"

"Same old, same old. Why you hanging up here? Mama Jean would have a fit, this ain't your life cuz."

He was younger than me and I wasn't feeling the fact he was getting more money than me. I was trying to get to the money and the streets act like it was a secret formula to it. I was tired of people telling I didn't belong out here, they had no idea I was born for this.

"Cuz, I'm trying to get money just like you," I told him.

"Man you not ready to get this money like me. If I pull you in, the only way out is jail or hell my boy."

"Man whatever. Show me the money."

"Okay…okay," he rubbed his little bit of chin hairs.

"Met me tonight at "The Spot"."

"Alright cuz," we dapped before he ran across the street holding his pants up.

The remainder of the day I sold a few bags of weed before walking down to the club to meet up with my little cousin. It was packed for it to be Sunday, it was the usual hole in the wall club that takes your breath away from the time you walk in the door. You could smell the weed and cheap perfume. The DJ was playing the latest trap music, I bopped my head as I made my way through the club. A tug on my shirt caught my attention when I saw Chardonnay, she didn't even have on the same outfit from early today so she already had her mind made up that she was hitting the club.

"What you doing in here," she yelled over the music.

"Nah the question is, why are you in here. I'm trying to make some money," I told her.

"Well I wasn't about to sit in the house and wait on you," She flipped her weave and it hit me in the face. She attempted to curl it but due to the heat in the club her curls fell but it didn't take away from how pretty she was.

"Alright well stay where I can see you and we can leave in a few," I told her in her ear.

"Yea," she said before twisting off.

Chardonnay was probably up to no good, but I could never catch her. She had way more in her little apartment than I could afford so I knew she was doing something to get some money. I headed to the back to lean up against the wall and watch the scene. I was waiting on my cousin to come through, when Chardonnay started dancing and whispering in this dude ear. Everything in the club stood still as I watched her enjoy herself.

I pushed my way through the crowd until I reached Chardonnay and her male companion. She was so into the dance and twerking she didn't even see me standing there until she stood up completely and opened her eyes. Her eyes were glossy and I knew she had popped a molly or some type of drug.

"Excuse me partner," I said to the dude. "Let's go Chardonnay," I pulled her by her arm.

"Gavon let me go," she yanked her arm back.

"Chardonnay, don't try me in this club let's go." I picked her up and threw her across my shoulder as she beat me in my back.

"Where your keys at," I searched her little handbag for her car keys. There was no way I was gone let another man take advantage of her while she was in this state. He probably slipped it to her anyway. After getting her home and settled, I got a text from my cousin telling me I missed out on some money but he will get with me tomorrow.

I jumped in Chardonnay car and went home, I'll take it back in the morning or whenever she woke up from what she was on.

Alvin

"Hey Alvin, you feeling alright this morning?'

"I can't complain man, God woke me up and that's good enough for me," I replied to my barber. He was the only one that knew how to tape me up like I wanted. When he came in he was a young buck that reminded me of my son, so I took him under my wing.

"Mama Jean coming to see you today?"

"Yea, I'm getting cleaned up for her. Every time she come she doesn't like me to look like I'm in prison. So I have to clean myself up before she gets here and look presentable. But how you doing? You hanging in there?"

"Yea I'm good. I hate I'll never see my son again, but it's just something I have to deal with. It's all my fault," he explained.

He finished up and I prepped myself for my visit. Every time Mama Jean came to visit, I prayed I would walk through visitation and see Gavon sitting there with her. I laid on my bed waiting for them to escort me to visitation. I'd been locked down for a long time, if I didn't get pictures of Gavon I wouldn't know what he looked like, on all the pictures he would be hanging with the homies on the streets or with his girlfriend. I could tell he was headed down the wrong path. I tried writing letters but I never get a response, so I stopped trying.

"Alvin let's go," CO stated.

I got up from the bed and placed my hands to the door to get cuffed to walk to the visitation area. I smiled as Mama Jean sat in her usual spot looking around and shaking her head, I already knew she had prayed before she walked in here. She often said that she didn't want to take none of them spirits back to her house. She waited as the officer uncuffed me before she got up and squeezed me. I towered over her and she laid her head in my chest.

From our relationship you would think Mama Jean was my mother, but she was my wife's mother. I was thankful that she stayed in my life after being charged with my wife's murder. She would tell me how she believed me way before she knew what happened. She knew I loved her daughter and my son with every fiber in my being.

"Sit, sit because you know we don't have that much time," she said easing into her seat.

"How you been? How is Gavon," I inquired.

"I'm good as can be. Gavon is being Gavon. But don't worry about him, let God do what he gone do with Gavon. Either he's going to submit or get broke down, either way he will submit before it's over. Anyway so how are you son?"

"I'm hanging ma, that's all I can do in here. Read my bible, go to church and workout."

"Well I'm trusting God that some more evidence comes up from somewhere. You've given them enough of your time while the person that killed my daughter is still out there. We serve a big God baby."

I believed everything Mama Jean said but it was starting to look like I was going to die in this place. Visitation was over and she kissed my cheek and said a quick prayer before I left her standing there. I was caged up like some animal. I needed to get to my son for the streets sucked him in and he ended up just like me. I was never a part of the streets, I worked as a brick mason. The street life was more of my wife's thing. I missed her dearly, she was my high school sweetheart. Her brothers ran the streets and often she would need a little money so she would make a drop, or cook for them to make a quick buck. Once Mama Jean got a whiff of it and went on the block and beat both of her sons. I was locked back in my room with my wife on my mind. Often times I wish I had answers myself, my heart told me it was a setup or maybe someone was plotting on my wife's demise and pin it on me.

———————

I woke up sweating, my hands were shaking uncontrollably. I hated when I went to sleep thinking of her and wake up sweating dreaming of what happened that night. Holding on to my wife as she gargled blood and ran her hands over my face with her bloody hands. I went straight down to my knees to pray, I was locked up for the murder of one but the only person that should've been murdered that night was the dude that thought it was okay to break into my house and violate my wife while my two year old son was sleep in the next room.

I went from praying straight into my work out, I had a whole routine and when I went outside for my hour I spent that time running. Mama Jean taught me how to pray and the importance of reading my bible, it kept me stable mentally. I thought of killing myself just so I could be with my wife. Mama Jean explained to me that killing myself would not make me feel better but would only lead me straight to hell. I was already in hell locked up for the rest of my life. Every day I woke up I was losing hope on my case. I had a lawyer that believed I killed my wife, he sabotaged my case intentionally. I spent all my money on him, Mama Jean kept a few dollars on my books with her check but I didn't expect her to take care of me but she insisted. I was trying my hardest not to start a small hustle to get up some money for a lawyer. I needed somebody to hear me out, and pull my files.

Mama Jean

"What a friend we have in Jesus, all our sins and griefs to bear. What a privilege to carry, everything to God in prayer. Oh, what peace we often forfeit. Oh, what needless pain we bear. All because we do not carry, everything to God in prayer."

"Mama Jean! Where is Gavon?" Chardonnay stood in front of me with her hands on her hips.

"Baby, did you not just walk up here and see me having praise and worship? You didn't speak or nothing, who raised you? Now where was I...*Have we trials and temptations-.*"

"Um hello Mama Jean," Chardonnay said coughing. I stopped sweeping my porch and singing since she spoke like she should have when she walked up.

"Hey suga."

"Do you know where Gavon is?"

"Well of course I do. Don't you hear the lawn mower in the back yard? We don't lay around the house over here. That's why he got you. Mama Jean don't play that over here, now once he get done cutting the grass you can have him. You are more than welcome to stay and wait, but I'm gone put you to work around here. I hate for you to mess them pretty little curls you bumped in that blue hair of yours, but this work makes you sweat." I looked at Chardonnay up and down and she had on all these labels I hadn't never heard of.

I heard the lawn mower shut off and I knew Gavon was headed up front to empty the bag. He walked around front shirtless with all those dang gone tattoos on his chest and back. He had dreads just like his father, he had them tied up in a knot.

"What's up Chardonnay? Something wrong?"

She looked over at me like she wanted me to give them some privacy. I got my broom and kept right on sweeping my porch, she had the wrong one. This was my house, if she wanted privacy then she needed to go down the street to her little apartment and talk after he got done cutting this grass of course.

"I need something from you, but I'll wait until you get done. I'll text you," she smacked her lips at me and rolled her eyes. I wanted to get the stick of my broom and hit her on top of all that blue hair she had in her hair.

"That girl ain't no good for you boy," I sat in one of my rocking chairs.

"Mama Jean come on."

"Don't come on me. I know that type, you make me mad thinking I just don't like her but it's something about her Gavon. But you know what, I'll let you see. How much longer you got on the yard?"

"I'm done. You have anything else for me to do before I shower?"

"No, but I did want to talk to you." He emptied the contents on the corner and came back and placed the bag back on the lawnmower and put it back in the storage house before he came and sat next to me on the porch.

"What you want to talk about?"

"Your father," I said looking at him.

"Mama Jean please not again. I can't with you and him. How can you care about a man that killed your only daughter?"

"Gavon you were far too young to understand what happen that night. You can't always go by what the streets told you happened. Only people know what happen that night is the people that were there and God. The only way to know the truth is to go and talk to the person that knows the truth."

"He's not about to look me in my face and lie to me like he doing you. I'm good, all I need is you."

"You may only need me, but he needs you. Alvin was one of the hardest working men I knew.

Your mother wanted for nothing, it was your uncles that got her use to the fast money. You know the fast money you like to go out there and get. Your father never did that, he found the legal way to bring money to the table and take care you guys. It's okay, I'm not going to push the issue. I'll let God deal with this."

Gavon got up and went in the house. I got up and finished up my chores around the house before I started my dinner. I was going to cook some field peas and okra, fried chicken, rice and corn bread. I never let Gavon run those streets hungry, I knew my words weren't going in one ear and out the other. I trusted God to send someone to water what I planted in Gavon. I was not your ordinary grandmother, I made sure I anointed him and prayed over him. He hated for me to put that oil on him. It was the oil that has kept him safe and out of harm's way all this time. My son's and their boys were out in the streets heavy. They were only welcome here to get something to eat, I didn't want that heat around my house. I blame them for their sisters' death and my son in law sitting in prison.

"Mama Jean I'll be back to eat. Let me go see what Chardonnay want."

"Hold on come here, I got a funny feeling. Let me go get my oil so I can pray for you," I left the kitchen heading for my room.

"Nah, Mama Jean. I'm just going up the road, I'll be back for dinner." He kissed my forehead and walked out the door. I had a feeling he wasn't going to make it back tonight. I went and stood to the screen door and watched as he walked down towards Chardonnay's apartment. I knew we stayed in the hood but where she stayed was like the projects. I went in sat in my chair and grabbed my bible. My grandson was my responsibility as long as Alvin was behind bars, I was not about to lose him. I had already lost my sons and other grandchildren to the fast life, that was not Gavon's life and I just wanted him to realize it before I lost him for good.

Chasiti

I only had a few more hours before it was time for me to clock out and go home. Although I loved my job I couldn't wait to get off of this fourteen hour shift. I had been here since three this afternoon but one of my coworkers had to leave early and asked if I could cover her last two hours. I didn't mind because whenever I needed her Samantha was right there to cover me.

I checked in on the patient that was in front of me before her husband took her to the labor and delivery floor. It was amazing watching her be so calm in full blown labor but she was still cracking jokes with her husband. The love they held for one another was evident in their eyes as they laughed and waited for me to be done. Come to find out this was their fourth child so she was used to it. I couldn't wait to become a wife and a mother one day.

Handing them their registration papers to sign, I made copies and asked her if everything was correct on her hospital bracelet before I placed it around her wrist. Once she confirmed the information I hit the button to open the door so they could head to the back corridor that would lead them to the Women's Tower.

"Congratulations again Mr. and Mrs.

Donovan. I'm sure this little blessing will add so much joy to your lives along with your other children," I said as they walked past me.

"Thank you so much sweetie. One day soon you will be experiencing this feeling with your husband," Mr. Donovan replied with a big smile on his face.

"Oh I'm not married yet," I said to him. I was a traditional type of girl. I wanted the husband and then the baby to follow. I already had a wonderful career that I loved and couldn't wait to share that one day with the man that God had for me.

"That's ok. God said to tell you that He was on his way so be ready," Mrs. Donovan smiled. I didn't even respond. I had heard that so much from the "church folks" that I stopped believing it after a while. Don't get me wrong, I knew that God had someone for me but I didn't think it would be this soon. I was only twenty four so I still had some youth to me before I would start worrying if I was going to get hitched or not.

I watched them as they went through the last set of double doors and could still hear their laughter. Just as fast as their laughter came and went as I heard a lot of commotion coming from the other end of the hallway. I turned to look behind me and noticed the doors opening in the ambulance bay and the red lights flashing. I knew this was serious because everyone was running around trying to get the patient that had just been brought in to the Trauma room in record time.

As a patient representative I was going to have to get as much information on him as possible so that I could get him registered as well as contact his next of kin if needed. I ran to get my portable computer so that I could try and register the patient. Once I saw the police coming in I knew that it would be a few minutes' maybe even hours before I would get a chance to fill out any paperwork.

There wasn't anyone in the waiting room right now because everyone in the Emergency Room had been either released or still being seen in the back so I had time to wait around to get what I needed. I saw that I had a text from my grandfather checking to make sure that I had made it home already. I loved my grandfather more than anything. He was the head pastor over at Greater Baptist here in Georgia and everyone loved and respected him. I would come to visit for the summer throughout my childhood and once I finished college I decided to move here to be closer to him and help out at his church.

Papa: Hey sweets! You make it home alright?

Me: No Papa I had to cover someone else's shift for a few more hours but I'll be home soon.

Papa: OK Sweets let know when you make it home.

Me: I will.

I giggled at the thought of my grandfather texting me. He had just learned how to use his new touch screen phone only a little while ago and now he couldn't stay off of it once I taught him how to use it. Don't get me wrong Papa or Reverend Rockmore wasn't that old but he was old enough that he had one of those Jitter Bug phones with the big buttons. I came home one weekend and almost went into cardiac arrest from laughing so hard at him and that phone. Once I got myself together I took him to go purchase a more up to date one that he automatically fell in love with.

As soon as I placed my phone in my sweater pocket I heard the all familiar sound of the heart monitor that was used to register a patient's heart rate start beeping uncontrollably.

"WE'RE LOSING HIM!" I heard Dr. Austin yell to the techs and nurses surrounding him. They began frantically moving around trying to get the defibrillator ready to shock the man on the stretcher.

"CLEAR!" I heard right before the sound of the machine sent I don't know how many volts of electricity through this man's body. All I could do was close my eyes and say a quick prayer on his behalf. I didn't know why I felt such a strong urge to pray out loud. I usually said a silent one for each patient that came through those doors when I was here but I was led to do it aloud.

"Amen." I heard a few of the other nurses

and some of the police men say once I was done.

"He's back!" I heard another one of the trama doctors say as the heart monitor started its steady beep. I had not realized I had been holding my breath until that moment I released it.

"Mr. Cunningham you gave us quite a scare there," Dr. Austin said.

Cunningham? Where had I heard that last name before? I knew it was familiar I just couldn't put my finger on it. I grabbed my computer to see if I could locate if the name was put into the system already so that I could get registration started since my shift was about to be over. I knew how hard it was sometimes getting the information when police were on the scene so if I didn't have to talk to them to get it my job was made easier. I typed in the last name and as soon as the information popped up on my screen I was about to be the next person to flat line when I saw that it was Mama Jean's grandson Gavon.

Mama Jean

My house phone startled me out of my sleep and I immediately turned to look at my clock. The time read 12:21am. Now I was old school and I didn't play about my phone ringing all types of night. I even made Gavon turn his cell phone down after a certain time. I got up off of my spot on the couch and walked over to the end table that sat on the other side of the den. Looking at the caller ID I saw a number that I was all too familiar with and knew doggone well this better not be no shenanigans.

"White wine, I mean Chardonnay I know good and well you not calling my house this late for no Gavon!" I said a little louder than normal. It was something about this Lil strumpet I just didn't like.

"Mama Jean" was all she said before she broke down crying. Before I could find out what this child's problem was there was a loud knock followed by someone ringing my bell uncontrollably.

"Jean it's Reverend! Jean! Open the door we gotta get to Gavon!" Lord knows that was all that I needed to hear. I forgot about Chardonnay on the phone as I dropped it and moved as fast as my knees would allow me to. I swung open the door with tears in my eyes.

"Where's my baby Mitch? Don't tell me my baby dead." I put my hand over my heart and prayed my pacemaker could hold on with whatever was said next.

"No he's not dead but we need to get to him

now." I didn't ask any more questions I just got to praying. I knew when that boy left earlier that he shouldn't have gone. It was so deep in my spirit but he was his mother's child and his uncle's nephew. Just hard headed.

Mitch got my purse out of my room and the house keys off of the table by the door and locked up as he helped me to his car. Once he got in and we were buckled I was hitting him with question after question.

"Mitch what happened? Is my baby ok? How do you know something was wrong with him? God knows I told him not to leave and go to that girl's house." It was at that moment that I realized I had left that girl on the phone when I dropped it to the floor. What ever happened I knew her fast behind had something to do with it.

"I don't know all of the specifics but Sweets

called me and told me he had just been brought in and it didn't look good." Sweets was what he called his granddaughter Chasiti. She worked down to the hospital on second shift.

"Lord keep my baby in your arms. Cover him and bring him out of this a better man. He still has work to do for your Kingdom." I said out loud. "He will be alright Jean," was all that Mitch said the rest of the drive there.

———————

I almost fell out of the car once it made a complete stop in front of the hospital emergency entrance. God knows I wish I was a little younger and still able to move like I used to. Once inside I headed straight to the information desk but before I could speak with the lady behind the desk Chasiti came running over to us.

"He's back here Mama Jean," she said holding the door open for us to enter.

"What happened Sweets?" Mitch asked as he held her close to him while he kept my hand in his. Lord this was not the time for me to be feeling all fuzzy inside but this was a fine old geezer here!

"They wouldn't tell me much since I'm not immediate family and all I know is he was stabbed. He died once but they were able to revive him."

"Oh heavenly Father!" I cried. My heart couldn't take losing someone else. I had already lost my daughter and my sons to the streets and Alvin was behind bars. I couldn't lose my baby boy Gavon too. So many nights I cried and prayed that things would be different for him but these days I wasn't too sure anymore.

"Here comes his doctor now."

"Is this the family of Gavon Cunningham?" Dr. Austin asked walking over to us. I was so distraught all I could do was nod my head.

"Yes this is his grandmother," Mitch said for me.

"And you are?" he asked Mitch.

"I'm their Reverend. Reverend Mitchell Rockmore."

"Is it OK if I speak with you in front of them?" he asked me and again all I could do was nod and hold on for dear life.

"Well Gavon is a strong young man. He was stabbed a total of eight times and lost a lot of blood," he explained.

"Oh Jesus no." I started crying uncontrollably just thinking about him going through so much pain.

"Will he be ok?" Chasiti asked.

"We lost him once on the way in route here and again a little while ago but he is stable now. The knife missed quite a few vital organs and thankfully he didn't slip into a coma. He needed a blood transfusion and it was nothing but God that Miss Rockmore here was the same blood type for Gavon. We didn't have time to wait to see if the lab had enough blood and had it not been for her we may not have been able to get him stable as quick. We are going to keep him for a few days but he will be fine and have no complications from this," he finished.

"Praise God!" I said as I cried tears of joy.

"I too had a praying grandmother. Keep doing it for him and he'll surrender in due time," Dr. Austin said surprising me. It wasn't too often when you heard people freely speak about prayer and God these days. It felt like a taboo subject so when you knew the care you were receiving came from a believer it made the situation a little easier to handle.

"Thank you so much Doctor." I managed to get out before my heavenly language took over and the tears flowed freely. The confirmation I needed to know that my baby would be OK was just given and I was overjoyed.

"You're very welcome. If you need me please don't hesitate to have me paged. Once he's in a room you all can go in and see him."

"Yes sir we will." Mitch said as he shook Dr. Austin's hand.

Before she knew what was happening, I had taken Chasiti into my arms and began thanking her for saving Gavon's life. Had she not been there I hated to think what would have happened.

Gavon

At last I was finally alone in my room. So much had happened in these last few hours and I couldn't make sense of it all. The last thing I remembered was leaving Grandma's house to go lay-up with Chardonnay before hitting the streets with my partner. I had come up on a lick and was about to make good on it. I was about to be straight for a long time. Next thing I know the door bursts open, she screams, and before I could turn around I'm being stabbed from all sides it seemed. Before I blacked out I heard her calling my name while on the phone with 911.

I didn't know if I was dreaming or if it was real but I saw my mother's face before me. She was beautiful.

Her jet black natural curly hair was in a neat afro, she had on an all-white dress that came down to her cute little feet. I remembered as a child when I would see my dad tickling her feet and she would laugh uncontrollably. That same smile she had on her face then she wore now.

The closer I got to her the further she would step back and her eyes held a sadness in them.

"Not now son," simply said. I wanted so bad to be with her again. Ever since her death my life hadn't been the same and I knew it was because she wasn't here. It's as if she was reading my mind when she said, "Your life doesn't stop because I am gone physically. I will never leave you Gavon."

I could feel the tears stinging my face and all I wanted was for my mother to hold me.

"But I need you mama," I cried out for her.

"Forgiveness is not for the other person it's

for you. Forgive baby," she said as she started to fade away from me slowly. God knows I didn't want her to leave and I didn't understand what she was talking about.

The last thing she said to me before she completely vanished was "It's not his fault."

"MAMA! MAMAAAAAA!" I screamed right before it felt like I was being electrocuted and my insides were set on fire.

I was brought back to the present when my room door opened and my Mama Jean came through followed by Reverend Rockmore and an angel. She looked familiar but I couldn't remember her name for the life of me.

"My baby," Mama Jean said before she gave me one of the most painful hugs ever.

"Jean you're hurting him," Reverend said.

"He's lucky I don't go get a switch off one of

those trees and wear his behind out right now! Scaring me half to death!" she fussed as she continued to kiss my face. "Didn't I tell you not to go? Lord you so hard headed!"

I wasn't even mad all I could do was smile because I knew she still loved me.

"Come on now Mama Jean you know thugs don't die," I said giving her the best smile that I could under the circumstances.

"Now you sound like a new school fool! Hmph baby everybody gonna have their day. Thugs and all but you better be worried about when it's your time where that soul of yours is gonna end up," Mama Jean stated seriously. I knew deep down she may have been right but I still had time to get myself together.

"I'm just glad you're Ok Gavon," the pretty angel said.

"Thanks ma," I said giving her my signature smile.

"I haven't had the time to officially introduce you to my granddaughter Chasiti. Each Sunday you run up out of church so fast I can't catch you," Reverend Rockmore laughed.

"My fault Rev." Had I known she was there maybe I would fellowship a little longer after service.

"Oh my God baby are you ok?" Chardonnay came rushing in.

I could see the Reverend shake his head and Mama Jean cut her eyes so hard Char should have dropped dead where she stood. My grandma knew she couldn't stand this girl but she was bae.

"Now chile it's too late for you to be coming up in here making all of this noise. It's other people in here that are sick and shut in. You could have a least glued that loose blue track back on ya scalp before you came in here." Mama Jean said and Chasiti tried her best to hold her laugh in. I couldn't lie Grandma was a trip and didn't care what she said sometimes. Chardonnay was so embarrassed as she raised her hand to try and tuck that track under another one. It didn't work though.

"I'm glad that you're feeling better though Gavon. It's past my shift being over so I'm going to head home now," Chasiti said and I couldn't help but smile at her. She was just naturally gorgeous. Her hair was cut into a cute little curly Mohawk style, her eyes were the color of milk chocolate and her skin was a golden color. She had a little mole on the left side of her cheek and a deep dimple on the right. Normally I wasn't attracted to thicker girls but she was definitely a breath of fresh air.

Before I could respond Chardonnay was

walking over towards her and her concerned demeanor had changed drastically. Instead of Chasiti looking intimidated she held her position and shifted her weight to her left leg and eased her arms across her chest. She had a lil feisty side to her and I liked that already.

"Who are you?" Chardonnay asked with that ratchet attitude I sometimes hated. She didn't know when to pull back sometimes and Mama Jean couldn't stand it.

"Chasiti. And you are?" she asked sweetly with a hint of "This ain't what you want" in her voice.

"She's also the one who saved his life," Mama Jean said confusing me.

"Huh? Mama what you tawm bout?" I asked.

"Chasiti was the only one who had your

blood type in order to give you a blood transfusion. Had it not been for her you could have gone into a coma and may not have made it out." she informed me smiling. You could see all of her brand new dentures with the gold caps on two of the teeth. She swore her little old self was fly and I couldn't lie she was.

"Oh word?" I said looking over to her as she blushed a little. Chardonnay took note of that and I swear that I saw smoke come from her ears.

"It was the least I could do and God lead me to do it. I'm just glad I was here and I could help," Chasiti stated. The more I looked at her the more something in me took control.

"I appreciate it for real shawty. That's what's up." I told her.

"Umm hello? I know yall not flirting like I'm invisible." This girl was a trip.

"Naw you not invisible but that part should be," Mama Jean cracked. This time Chasiti couldn't help but laugh out loud and so did I.

"Jean!" Reverend said.

"Whet?" she replied sounding like Chardonnay.

"We will let you get some rest and be back later on. I'm just glad that you're OK son." he said to me.

"Preciate that Rev." I said as he tapped my shoulder. Before they left he said a quick prayer of covering and healing over me that I was grateful for.

As soon as they left Chardonnay went in.

"So you get out of the bed with me and now you laid up smiling in the next chick's face like I'm not standing right here?"

"Hold on fam. Instead of you worried about

how I'm doing after I got stabbed at your house, you worried about the next broad? Wow." I said finding myself getting heated when something crossed my mind.

"How did I get stabbed anyway? I know when I came in I locked the door behind me and I don't remember hearing anyone break in on us. So what's good?" I asked her. The look on her face let me know something was up but I wasn't gonna call her out on it just yet. One thing I heard faithfully from Mama Jean was that everything that was done in the dark would surely come to the light.

Chardonnay

This was not the way this was supposed to be going. The only reason I was even here was because I didn't want it to look suspect if I didn't show up concerned but once I saw Miss Thickums up here smiling and being all cute in my man's face I got sidetracked.

I was only here to see what Gavon remembered and to make sure that no faces were seen. Gavon wasn't a real street cat and he always got caught slipping. You would think that after getting stolen from or caught up so many times by the real G's in the hood he would give it up. He had heart though because he kept going but he wasn't bout that life for real and everybody knew it but him.

"What are you talking about bae?" I said getting back into character of the distraught girlfriend.

"You hear me?" He said trying to sound gangster. He didn't even have enough bass in his voice. Gavon looked the part all day with the tats, long dreads, and the fronts in his mouth but as soon as you saw him in action it was a wrap.

He didn't know that I knew about him only getting 5g's for a lick he hit with his partner Po Cat the other night. They got away with over 50k and he let Po only give him five. No real street dude would have let that happen on the real.

"Maybe I didn't lock the back door. I remember it being open earlier and when I closed it I can't recall locking it." I said. I knew full well I didn't lock it because that was the only way that my plan would go off without a hitch.

"Bae how many times do I have to remind you to be careful? You are a woman and I may not always be there to protect you." he said like he would bust anything besides a grape. Gavon couldn't even hold a gun right when he got shook.

The only little clout he got was on the strength of his late mother and his uncles. If it wasn't for them he would have been so green to the underworld. Gavon tried his best to follow in their footsteps but everybody wasn't built for this life.

"You right and I'll try to be more careful. I was so scared and worried about you. To come out the bathroom and see you in all of that blood almost killed me." I lied. I had gone into the bathroom after a love session with Gavon and sent a text to Mario letting him know he could come in. I turned the shower on and cracked the door when I heard Gavon yell. It was after that I ran out and put on one of the best acting performances ever. Screaming and hollering like my life depended on it, and in a way it did. More about that later right now I needed him to believe me and I knew the perfect way.

I walked over to him and gave him one of the most passionate kisses I had ever given him. Don't get me wrong I loved Gee but he wasn't hood enough for me. He really did belong in a church somewhere passing out funeral home fans and tithing envelopes not trying to hit a lick for a come up.

As I thought about it this new chick was going to be a problem. Gee may have a calling on his life but I wasn't about to let him answer that one. I could tell little Miss Thang would be the one to open his eyes and although he wasn't hood enough for me I wasn't giving him up. We weren't married but it was til death did us part. Literally.

Gavon

Chardonnay must've thought I was a fool. No matter how people thought I wasn't from the streets, one thing they couldn't take away from me was my common sense. This is where Chardonnay messed up at, while she was playing the innocent girlfriend I could see right through her little façade. That same dude she was twerking on was the same dude that set me up. See while I was leaning on the wall that night at the club watching my surroundings, dude was watching me too. I had seen Chardonnay whispering in his ear and everything that night; it was only when she started dancing on him that got me heated. In the meantime I was gone sit back and chill and act like I was clueless. I hit my morphine drip one last time before I fell into a deep sleep.

The screams of my mother woke me up out of my sleep. Placing my little teddy bear out of my arm and putting in the bed, I turned over and slid out the bed until my little feet hit the floor. I pushed my little step stool up to the door to open it when a shot went off. I jumped down and covered my ears because they were now ringing. After a few seconds later another shot went off, I could hear my daddy screaming my mother's name telling her to wake up. I got back up on my stool and twist the door knob, once I got it open I moved the stool and walked out into our living room where I saw my father covered in blood and holding my mother in his arms crying and kissing her face.

"Gavon go back to your room!" He yelled. I was young but I was not your average two year old. Once he noticed I wouldn't leave he laid my mother down softly and came over to me and kneeled down. And kissed me and told me how much he loved me. He grabbed my hand and walked me back to my room and placed me in my bed, before walking out. I never saw him again.

———

"Wake up sleepy head," Mama Jean said. Waking up seeing her was what I needed after a dream like that, I needed some answers.

"Hey Mama Jean, what you doing up here so early?"

"Boy it's not early. Let me get the nurse and tell her to take you off this morphine cause you losing you mind," she stated.

"Whatever," I laughed.

"So now that everything has calmed down, what happened?" she asked the dreadful question I didn't want to answer until I had all the answers.

"I can't really remember," I lied. The look she gave me let me know that she knew I was lying as well.

"Mmhhmm, lying thing you. You gone keep right on and your little ghetto girlfriend gone make sure you dead, coming in here with all that acting. I'm not any old fool. Keep her from round my house before I hurt her," Mama Jean said angrily.

"I got you."

"You better understand me; because I'm gone hurt her feelings."

"Mama Jean what happen the night my mother got murdered?"

"Gavon, I wasn't there but I think that's something you need to talk to your father about."

"That's okay, I don't ever want to see or talk to him."

"Gavon you have a lot of growing up to do, until you sit and talk to him you will never understand what happened that night. Now since we were doing all this talking your grits getting cold. You know I'm not gone have you up here eating this nasty hospital food, chile please." She unwrapped the plate which had bacon, grits, eggs and raisin toast. Mama Jean was so old fashion with all these grocery store bags she placed my food in. I still was in a lot of pain so sitting up too much caused too much pain so I had to slouch and eat my food.

"How you feeling today?" the doctor came in and asked.

"I'm in pain," I winced.

"That's expected young man. I tell you, you are going to have one heck of a testimony. Eight stab wounds all missing vital organs. I can only pray you are connected to a church somewhere. I'm going to get the nurse in here to change those bandages and look at your wounds so we can decide when we will let you go home," he pulled the cover back up over my stomach.

Mama Jean stayed until they changed my bandages. She said she needed to go home and cook dinner and she would be back to bring me a plate.

"Gavon," I heard my name being called

from the door. I didn't know who the voice belonged to so I had to wait until they came around the curtain. Right now I didn't trust anyone but Mama Jean and I meant to tell the staff not to let anyone in my room but Mama Jean. I changed my mind when Chasiti came from around the curtain in her work clothes. We smiled at each other.

"Hey come in," I tried my best to sit up and man up.

"No…no lay down," she rushed over and helped me get comfortable.
"Thank you ma."

"I'm glad you're up. Yesterday I didn't know if you were going to make it," she stated.

"I wouldn't be here if it wasn't for you. Again I preciate it."

"That's what Christians do," she said sitting on the side of my bed. I wasn't sure what she meant by Christians but if that's what she was I wanted in on it.

"Let me apologize for my girlfriends' behavior on yesterday as well."

"No need to apologize for her. I don't let people like her bother me, she's very insecure."

I was shocked little mama was so spunky, most thick chicks weren't very confident but she had her swag about her. She didn't come off as street or hood, she was already established and I liked that about her.

"Well I just came to check up on you on my lunch break, I'll be getting off soon. Hopefully they will let you out so we can see you in church Sunday."

"I hope so too, if not just come chill with me until they do," I smiled at her.

"Alright," she smiled and waved.

Chasiti

I made it to the end of my shift, it took everything in me not to go back upstairs and check on Gavon. I couldn't focus on anything, just thinking about him. I hope I wasn't starting to feel him like that; his look didn't match what I had seen on the inside. I guess I understand now what God meant when he said He judges a man on their inner appearance and we judge by the outside. Not saying his dreads weren't nice and his nose ring complimented his look as well. I desired to be married and have kids but every guy I dated had an ulterior motive. I was still a virgin and I didn't plan on giving myself to anyone until I was married.

"Hey Sweets," my papa spoke into the phone.

"Hey Papa, I was just letting you know I made it home safe."

"Ok good now I can rest, I hate you work that shift. Late night Savannah is not the safest."

"Yea I know. But I love what I do Papa," I explained.

"I understand. Did you go check on Mama Jean's grandson today?"

"Yes sir. He's doing better than he was doing yesterday I can tell you that."

"That's good to hear. If he gets out of there in time and makes it to church on Sunday I want to invite to dinner that evening at my house."

"Oh okay no problem," I swallowed hard.

"Why do I hear apprehension in your voice sweets?"

"Nothing Papa, it's just that I don't think he's the type to bring around that's all," I said trying to convince my own self. I was scared to fall for his type but I was definitely falling hard and fast.

"None sense chile! I see a lot further than you see and I know what God is about to do in his life. Sweets don't judged him by what you see, he has a great potential."

"I didn't mean it like that Papa," I stressed.

"I know you didn't," he chuckled. "I'll talk to you tomorrow make sure to lock up before you go to bed," he said before we hung up.

I showered and ate a bowl of Ramen noodles before laying down to catch up on the shows I'd missed due to work. My phone signaled letting me know I had a Facebook message, it was strange because I hardly ever got on Facebook because it was full of drama but I had it to keep up with the parents of the church. I popped my lips and rolled my eyes when I saw who the message was from.

Chardonnay WineFine has sent you a message: Hey I was just wanting to let you know that our little run in we had last night is over as long as you stay away from Gavon. We appreciate you for saving his life and all but don't for once think that we owe you anything. Tootles Chardonnay

I was now convinced that the girl was crazy. I laughed at her profile picture which was a picture of her shooting a bird and showing her tongue ring. She was pathetic, I had no problem staying away from Gavon. I didn't want anyone's man, God promised me my own one day and I believed God was going to do just that. I shut my phone off without so much as a reply and went to bed. I was off the next day and I didn't plan on leaving the house unless my Papa asked me to do something for the ministry.

Just like I thought, first thing this morning my Papa was asking me to do something for the ministry. Of course I didn't mind at all though. I ran the daycare for the church sometimes when Mrs. Greta couldn't and I was not working at the hospital. I had a few things I needed to pick up, I just didn't want too. I wanted to sleep in just a little longer but I guess the old saying rang true, I could sleep when I was dead. I finally got up to shower and dress myself. I got my black sweats, my favorite red UGA t-shirt, threw a Georgia hat on my head and put on my Nike slides and headed out the door to Target.

After picking up some wipes and hand sanitizer for my class along with a few other things I went and got the stuff for Papa as well before heading to the check-out line.

"Yea this fat chick called herself giving Gavon some blood to save his life. She thinks she just gone come in and take my man, I've invested too much time in Gavon to let some fat broad take him from me," I stood behind Chardonnay as she yapped on her phone about me. She had a fresh sew in, I mean I would too if Mama Jean put me on blast. The bob was bad, I just didn't understand why she picked the colors she did. I cleared my throat to let her know someone was standing behind her. She turned around and noticed it was me and hung her phone up without even saying goodbye to her caller.

"Hi Chardonnay," I waved.

"Hey," she said dryly. It was funny that she was here by herself and she was quiet now that I was in her presence but was just talking a lot of trash on the phone. I didn't even bother to mention that I heard her whole conversation.

"Next," the cashier yelled out. Chardonnay placed all her items on the counter and paid for them.

"It was good seeing you again. Um, I didn't get your name."

"Chasiti is the name, but you knew that yesterday. So please stop referring to me as the "fat chick". I said to her as she rolled her eyes and walked off. I laughed on the inside. She was going to be the downfall of Gavon if he didn't watch out.

Chardonnay

"Chardonnay you got to be the dumbest chick I know!" Mario yelled.

"I'm getting dressed now to go check on him dang. You don't have to do all that yelling," I said slipping on some jeans and a shirt.

"How you only seen him once since he been up there? He gone know you up to something. Its bad enough he survived after all those jabs I gave him. I'll be back later on," Mario said with a hard scowl on his face while putting his fitted cap on and headed out the door.

I ran my fingers through my green and blue weave and put some gloss on before getting in my car and heading to the hospital. I wasn't in the mood to fake with Gee today. My love for him had long ago faded once I realized he wasn't getting no real money. Parking my car in the visitors section I got out and headed inside. I popped my strawberry gum as I made my way up to his door and heard Mama Jean's voice. I stomped my foot like a little school girl because I really had to put on now.

"Hey baby how you feeling," I ran in kissing him all over his face.

"Unt uh unt uh baby, don't come in here kissing on him like that. Where your lips been?" she asked looking over the top of her glasses.

"Whatever," I waved her off. She was always coming for me she just don't know I wanted to slap them gold caps out of her mouth.

"I'm good. The question is where you been for two days?"

"I was out trying to find a job. I'm trying my best to change, because that's all you complain about." I lied. There was no way I was punching someone else's clock to get paid when there were men waiting to keep me laced.

"That's good to hear ma. Well I should be out of here by tomorrow, you gone come get me?"

"No, you coming home so you can heal properly. Why would you want to go back to the place where you got stabbed Gavon?" Mama Jean asked.

"Mama it's okay. I'll be home I just had something I needed to get from Chardonnay's house that's all," Gee explained.

"Alright! Now if you ain't home by the time I turn my stove off tomorrow night, I'm coming down there to get you. Now I'm gone give you some privacy because you grown, but Chardonnay I'm gone tell you to your face that I don't trust you. My grandson almost died in your apartment, something real fishy smelling to me but for the sake of him I'm gone let God handle you." she said sending a chill down my spine. Although I was shook she would never know it.

Gee and I watched as Mama Jean grabbed her old brown purse that probably weighed more than her and walked out with her bad knees.

"What is her deal with me Gee?" I asked as

if I didn't know.

"That's my grandma man, she's protective. Anyway where did you go looking for a job at today?"

"I've been so many place I can't even remember," I lied again. Gee was always pushing for me to find a job and become more independent. What I look like working for somebody else, I looked too good for that.

"Bae you ever thought about going to school?"

Gee didn't know this but I didn't even have my high school diploma. I dropped out my 12th grade year because I rather stay home then for someone to tell me what to do. I had a serious problem with authority, this is the reason I plan stuff and then hide because I knew if I ever ended up in jail it was going to be a serious problem. As a matter of fact I would rather die before I go to jail.

I sat around with Gee with about thirty minutes, I really wasn't paying him attention because I was too busy looking up this Chasiti chick on Facebook that was intruding in my life. She was real cute for a thick chick, I couldn't even front, but she had nothing on me. I wrapped my gum around my finger as I started plotting on little miss perfect. She had all these encouraging quotes on her page and pictures of her at church and in the nursery with the kids. Just the thought of her giving Gee her blood upset me, because now I felt like they had a deeper connection than he and I.

"Alright Gee I'm about to head home before it gets too late," I got up and kissed him on his lips. I wanted to puke when he tried to kiss me deeper. Don't get me wrong, Gee was a sight to see, he just wasn't it for me. But in order to take him for everything he didn't even know he possessed, I had to act like I was so in love with him.

"You just got here." he said looking up at me.

"I know but I need to do a little running around and I don't want to be out late."

"Well text me once you make it home."

"Yea," I said as I slipped out the door. I headed downstairs and asked the lady a few questions about Chasiti, she only gave me her next work day which was fine with what I had planned for her.

I got back to my apartment and Mario was already there watching my tv, eating my food and sucking up my air. If he wasn't bringing in the money to pay these bills and keep me laced like I needed, he wouldn't be here either.

"Mario we got a problem," I pushed his feet off my table. I may have stayed in the projects but I made sure when you stepped in here it was clean. Gee made sure I had some of the best furniture and accessories with his little coins.

"What now," he asked.

"It's this chick named Chasiti that's works at the hospital where Gee's at. She gave him some of her blood so he could live. The problem is I can tell they feeling each other and I'm not feeling that at all," I said with an attitude.

"If I didn't know any better I would think you were jealous of her." Mario said making my blood instantly begin to boil. I may not have wanted Gee much longer but I wasn't about to let Miss Saved and Sanctified have him.

"Whatever man. Find out some info on her and let me handle it," he said making me smile again.

"I have her schedule if that would help."

"That's perfect," he said showing his mouth full of golds.

Gavon

Today was my release day, Mama Jean had called to try and convince me to let her or Rev pick me up but I kindly reminded her that Chardonnay was coming to get me. She had an attitude about it but promised to have a nice hot meal ready for me when I got home. The only reason I had Chardonnay coming to get me was because I wanted to do a walk-through of what happened that night. It was strange she all of a sudden had to use the bathroom and any other time she left the bathroom door open, but that night she closed and locked it.

"Hey you, Chasiti said.

"Hey beautiful," I smiled at her causing her to blush.

"I see you heading home huh," she said sounding somewhat sad.

"Yea but it's not like you will never see me again. I'm out just in time to go to church in the next few days." I told her smiling. This girl was doing something to me and I didn't know how to feel about it.

"Speaking of church. My papa wants to invite you over for dinner Sunday if you are able to sit up long enough." she informed me.

"No doubt, I can join you guys for dinner. I may have to dip out early though to meet up with my people." I said limping over towards her as she frowned at me.

"Okay I'll make sure to let him know," she said turning to walk back out.

"Hold up! Listen how can I repay you for saving my life?" I asked. I didn't want her leaving me just yet.

"It's nothing, like I said before it's what I was supposed to do anyway."

"But I feel like I owe you though,"

"I tell you what. If you promise to not go back to what caused you to come in here is good enough for me." she said putting it out on the table. She actually cared, I put my head down because I couldn't make that promise to her just yet.

"I don't know about all that." I honestly told her.

"Why not?" She asked with obvious frustration in her voice.

"Come on ma. You understand how this life goes. I won't rest til the person who tried taking my life is dealt with."

"That's just it. I don't understand why people just can't take situations and look at them as a wake up call from The Lord. He's trying to wake you up Gavon before it's too late." Chasiti was even more beautiful when she was mad.

"You know you sound just like my grandma." I scoffed. I wasn't trying to make her upset but it irked me when people tried to tell me how to live my life.

"Is that such a bad thing? Mama Jean is very wise and she loves you more than you know." She said walking over to me and holding my hand. Her skin touching mine felt so right and I didn't want the feeling to end.

"I'll try to do what you asked." I told her not a hundred percent sure that I could. But I didn't want her leaving upset. It was crazy how I never cared if Chardonnay and I fell out but God knows for some reason I felt like I had to protect Chasiti's heart.

"Ok so I'm going to hold you accountable to that. Give me your number so I can check in and make sure that you are staying on the right track," Chasiti said.

I limped over to the bed side table and gave her my phone so she could put her number in my phone instead.

"What are y'all doing?" Chardonnay appeared in the doorway and stood there with an attitude.

"Hey baby. I was getting Chasiti's phone number." There was no sense in lying when I was caught red handed. Chardonnay wasn't aware yet but this thing between us was over.

"So you switched to the thick side now? You are just plan out disrespectful. And you,"

Chardonnay pointed in Chasiti's face. "I'm getting sick of seeing you already. I've asked you politely to stay away from him." she said rolling her neck. If she rolled it any harder it was going to roll under the bed.

"Please move your finger out of my face," Chasiti said calmly.

"Or what?" Chardonnay moved in closer. I was in no predicament to break up a cat fight.

"Chardonnay chill out in these people hospital getting all loud. This girl works here."

"I DON'T CARE!" Chardonnay said loudly swaying back in forth. I see she was trying to get Chasiti upset but it wasn't working.

"Chasiti it was good seeing you again," I said trying to signal for Chasiti to leave.

"Same to you Gavon. Take care of yourself. I'll see you at church."

"Oh don't worry boo, I got him. You just gone on back downstairs to your measly job and tend to them folks and eat your Debbie cakes." Chardonnay sassed.

"See what you not gone do is disrespect me. I haven't come out the mouth at you yet. But I see you really trying to push my buttons…"

"HELP…HELP!" Chardonnay started screaming and everything causing the nurse to run in my room.

"What's the problem in here?"

"She slapped me," Chardonnay lied.

"Are you serious?! I didn't touch her," Chasiti explained.

After talking with Chasiti's supervisor and giving my side of the story, Chasiti was excused and had finally I was headed home with Chardonnay's crazy behind.

"Ma you were dead wrong for what you did," I mugged her.

So!" she yelled clearly not taking the situation seriously.

"So? That girl could have lost her job fooling around with you.

"Like I said before, so!"

I couldn't believe Chardonnay and her behavior. She was showing a side I knew she probably had but had never seen and I wasn't feeling it at all. Everybody knew she was ghetto but this jealous side of her was ridiculous. We pulled up into the apartment complex and once we entered her house I knew something was off. There was a scent of a man that lingered in the air, I smelled freshly smoked weed and I hadn't been here since the accident almost a week ago. Chardonnay hardly ever smoked so I knew it wasn't her. I could tell she tried to cover it up with her Hawaiian air freshener but that didn't work. My hair stood up on my arms as I walked pass the bathroom and into her room as that night came back to me clearly. I walked out of her room and into the kitchen to check the back door which was locked. *That's funny, it's locked today.* I walked in the bathroom and replayed the scene, the way the dude was dressed when he ran up on me reminded me of someone I had seen before. I couldn't even remember if I heard Chardonnay scream or not that night. As a matter a fact she didn't even come out the bathroom until after the stabbing when I know she heard the commotion. I came out of the bathroom and started gathering all my clothes and belongings that was at her house.

"What are you doing Gee?"

"Look this thing we got going on is over."

"Oh so now that this Chasiti chick done

came in your life, it's over? Gee you can never get rid of me. You just mad right now so I'm gone let you have it. But you'll be back," she laughed. I didn't find anything funny as I called Mama Jean to come pick me up.

Chardonnay ran and grabbed the bleach and started pouring it all over my clothes and shoes. A little bit of bleach splashed on one of my wounds and caused pain to shot down my side.

"So you think you just gone up and leave Chardonnay, you must be crazy!" She was jumping around looking like a mad woman. Hearing the horn to Mama Jean's car brought me back to reality.

I limped outside towards the door holding my side with my eyes burning from all the bleach Chardonnay had used.

"Boy what's wrong with you? And why you smell like a whole gallon of bleach?"

"I broke things off with Chardonnay and she decided to poor bleach all over my clothes and shoes."

"Wait, unt uh. No she didn't let me go talk to her cause see she playing with the right one. Where is my purse?" my grandma said trying to get out of her seatbelt with the car still in drive. She was about to send us both back yo the hospital if she didn't calm down.

"Mama Jean it's cool. She is not worth it. I got bigger and better things in store and she is not on the list. I'm just ready to go home and get in my bed."

As we were pulling off Chardonnay started throwing my stuff out in trash bags, shooting birds and everything.

"See she thinks I'm too old to get with her. But she got one mo time and I do mean one mo, and it's me and her. I'm gone wrap my fingers round up in that blue green hair and yank her! See now I got to ask the Lord to forgive me for them thoughts. That girl bring out the bad in me, that's why you got to stay from around her," Mama Jean stated.

Chasiti

I walked into the Five Guys and ordered the biggest burger on the menu. Because of Chardonnay I was suspended for five days. It was intentional and I saw through it but I didn't expect for her to scream. Had I known she was gonna do all that then I should have slapped her. I sat in a corner and pulled my phone out to read this good book on my Kindle. I heard about a new author from Virginia whose name was Tabeitha Pollard Mann so I downloaded her book *Done In The Dark*.

"Anybody sitting here?"

I looked up at the male and rolled my eyes. If it was anything I didn't like, it was for a man to see the seat across from me empty and invite himself to my table. I choose the back table so I wouldn't be bothered.

"No," I bit my burger.

"May I sit? I saw you over here by yourself. I thought maybe you wanted some company."

"To be honest I'm fine I don't need any company," I said harshly.

"Whoa, you are just brutal. I'm not trying to marry you. I was just wanting to know your name, you look like you could use a friend right now."

"My name is Chasiti and I'm not big on friends," I watched him.

"My name is Mario. It's nice to meet you Chasiti. Are you always this mean or have you had a rough day at work?"

"Something like that," I said a little softer.

"You want to talk about it?"

"Nothing to talk about, I got into it with a girl she lied and said I hit her, I got suspended and here I am."

"Wow, yea you had a horrible day. You should let me take you out," he smiled and I saw all of his golds.

"Nah, I don't hang out like that. I'm not your type. See I'm a church girl and I don't think you want me cramping your style like that." I told him.

See boys like Mario had a motive behind approaching an ordinary girl like me. He knew as well as I did that I was not his type and I didn't do well with playing games.

"I don't think you would cramp my style, I

think you would add to it. So what you think about dinner?"

He was so cute begging, and I knew he had never been with a girl like me. I gave it some thought while I finished my sandwich. My Papa taught me well and I knew how to handle myself so I didn't see anything with giving him a try. The only thing I could see wrong was his mouth, I wasn't fond of the golds in his mouth but he dressed well. I didn't want to prejudge him.

"Ok we can do dinner. We can meet about 8 tonight at Lady & Son's," I threw my demands out there. No he was not coming to my house and no he was not picking me up in his car. I didn't know him like that.

I wrapped myself in my towel and unraveled my towel off my hair. I let my hair fall on my shoulders, I looked in the mirror and tried to figure out how to wear my hair. I plugged my blow dryer up and connected the comb so I could detangle and dry it at the same time. After getting it blow dried I opt to just brush it into a ponytail. I didn't want to give him any idea that this was more than what it was. I put a little lip gloss on and some mascara. I put on my maxi dress and sandals and headed out the door.

I never went on a date without telling my Papa where I was going and who the guy was. He was very protective of who I dated. I didn't want him worrying so I shot him a text and told him I was going out to Lady & Son's and I would call him once I made it home. The restaurant was packed as I expected on a Friday night. I chose this because if I wasn't feeling him I could leave without worrying about him snatching me or going off. He hadn't made it yet so I had time to get myself together and say a quick prayer that God would protect me. Looking at me you would never know that I was shield from some many things because of my parents pass. Papa always thought that the enemy was after me because of the dark stuff my parents were in. Papa was able to get me out before I was old enough to understand about the calling on the dark world as my mother would call it. She was waiting for me to turn a certain age but Papa came to snatch me before I was 10.

"Hey Chasiti," Mario said pulling his chair out and sitting across from me. He handed me a dozen roses and a card. When he smiled he didn't have his mouth jewelry in which made him look more mature. He wore a nice button up shirt and crisp jeans, unlike earlier today he didn't have on his LeBron's. He now wore a pair of causal shoes. It was nice to see he adjusted his appearance which was a plus.

"Hey Mario." I greeted him with a smile. "You look nice," he complimented me.

"Thank you and you do as well."

"So what do you usually eat when you are here? I never been here before," he asked.

"I usually eat the buffet because of the options," I explained.

"Ok bet, let's do that."

After we ordered our drinks and walked to the buffet and fixed out plates we rejoined at the table. I waited to see if he would say his grace.

"Could you bow your head so I can bless the food?" he asked. I was really shocked.

I bowed my head and closed my eyes as he blessed the food. We ate and had a nice conversation but his phone kept going off and he got up a few times to talk on the phone. Now the first two times I excused him but after the third time I was becoming irritated so I got up and left without letting him know. I didn't have time to play and waste my time. Quickly I sent a text my Papa and let him know I was on the way home and would call him once I made it in. I didn't do well with games and that's what Mario was doing. By the time I made it home he had called twice. If he wanted to speak to me again he was gone have to bring his A game.

Chardonnay

"Are you going to let me do this or not?" Mario yelled in my ear. I removed my phone from my ear to make sure I had called the right person cause Mario knew I was not the one to play with.

"Ummm who you think you talking to?" I said as I popped my gum loud in his ear. He had me messed up.

"Chardonnay don't get messed up!" He warned. I knew when he got like this things wouldn't end well so I decided to leave this battle alone.

See Miss Thang thought that I didn't pick up on her trying to get close to my man. Always hanging around acting like she's concerned but I knew that was all a front. She was just trying to get close to him but I wasn't about to sit back and let that happen.

No I didn't want him but I be darn if I let someone else have him. Not after all of the years

I've invested. But I also knew that I couldn't get rid of her by myself so who better than to see help from than my baby daddy? That's right I was twelve weeks pregnant with Mario's baby and once we hit this major lick my baby and I would be set.

Gee didn't know that I was pregnant yet but he would soon find out and when he did I would have him eating out of the palms of my hands just like I had Mario and all I would have to do was enjoy it.

Gavon could play like he didn't have money but little did he know I knew otherwise. One of his uncles hung with my cousin's cousin and was always talking about how Gavon's daddy still had some of his late wife's money stashed away for him. Now no one really knew where it was or if was even true but something deep in my spirit told me that something may have been out there floating around and Mario and I wanted it.

"Dang man!" I heard Mario yell bringing me back to the present.

"What's wrong baby?" I asked sitting up in bed.

"She's gone."

"What do you mean she's gone Mario? What did you do!" I was panicking. I knew God probably wasn't listening to me but Lord please don't let this man be done killed this girl. I knew how his temper could get and if he didn't get his way he could snap just like that.

"Because you kept blowing me up like you crazy she probably got tired of me answering this phone and left. I told you I had everything under control," He fussed. I was just glad to know he hadn't hurt her. At least not yet.

Once I saw how Gavon and Chasiti looked at each other like they had a love connection so deep, I knew that she would be the one he left me for and I couldn't have that before I got a hold to that money. Once that happened I would easily get rid of him. Mario was supposed to step in, get close to her, and get her focus off of Gavon but something was telling me this wouldn't be easy. Mario wouldn't tell me what he planned on doing and that alone had me shook.

"I'm sorry baby. I was just nervous and wanted to know what was going on," I said trying to get him calm again. If he walked in this house mad at me because I messed this up it wouldn't be pretty for me. His hands were lethal and the last thing I wanted to do was lose this baby cause of one of his beatdowns.

"Yeah you're sorry alright and you're about to be sorrier once I get there. And you better be up when I get there," He said ending the call before I could respond. This night was about to get worse for me but I knew in the end these bruises and black eyes would be worth it.

Mama Jean

God knows He keeps His hands on my baby when he's out there in those streets. If I had lost him my life would have been over. No matter how much I stayed on my knees in prayer for my children to be changed it never happened. My daughter was murdered for the life she lived and my two sons

Danny and Reno had been turned over to a reprobate mind years ago. They cursed God so bad they were no longer welcomed in my home. Yes I loved my children but I loved my God more. That's why I knew He would deliver Gavon out of this hell he was living in on earth.

I knew that one of my babies was gonna have a chance. God had already showed me my baby boy would be alright so I wasn't even worried anymore. I just prayed that he didn't have to go through anymore suffering before his change came although something told me that would not be the case.

I looked up to see Gavon coming down the steps fully dressed. He still had that slight limp but he was looking stronger by the day. Glancing over to the time on the cable box I saw that it was going on eleven at night.

"Where you going so late? You know we got church in the morning," I said to him as I continued to study my word.

"I know mama. I won't be long I just need to go check on some things right quick."

"Don't be over there at that little strumpet's house. I know she had something to do with hurting you and I ain't never liked her no way. Little disrespectful wanch. Father forgive me and bridle my tongue Lord but you know I don't like that little fast girl. Hmph!"

"Nah I told you I'm done with her. I do have my eyes on someone else though." He told me and that lightened my mood.

"Yes Chasiti is a beautiful young woman. So smart and pretty. And my God her spirit is so pure." I said smiling.

"How you know that's who I'm referring too?" He asked me trying to hold his smile in.

"Baby this old coon here knows when love is in the air. I saw how you lit up when you found out she had given you that blood transfusion. And I also notice how you look at her the times that she is able to make it to church. It's all over your face," I schooled him.

"I was just thankful that's all," He said coming to kiss me on my forehead.

"Mmm hmm. Let me just tell you this. If you step to her you better step correct. Don't get involved with her if you can't leave these streets alone. She may seem tough but her heart is fragile and when she loves she loves hard. If you can't man up and be the man of God that she needs you to be for her you just move along. Do you hear me son?"

"Yes ma'am. I'll be back in a few." He said heading to the front door. I knew he was thinking about what I had said because the look on his face told it.

"Gavon?" I said right before he was able to walk out.

"Yes ma'am?"

"I'm going to see your father Monday morning," I said as I heard the door shut indicating he had gone.

"Lord touch his heart. He's gonna need his father more than ever in his life if he is going to make it out of these streets alive. Mend this broken relationship between father and son God. In Jesus name I pray, Amen."

This was going to be a fight here.

"I know good and well my phone is not ringing at three o'clock in the morning." I said as I sat up. Lord I had fallen asleep in my chair after Gavon left earlier. I prayed this wasn't another call about something happening to him.

Before I could reach the phone I saw the shoes he had worn when he went out by the front entrance and I sighed as relief came over me. Now whoever this was calling my house this late better have a good reason. I didn't even bother looking at the caller ID.

"To God be the glory," I answered trying to mask how I was feeling on the inside.

"Where Gavon at?" that little buzzard Chardonnay yapped in my ear.

"Lil girl I done told you about calling my house this late with your disrespectful, no home training having self. Gavon told you he didn't want nothing to do with you anymore. Don't call my house no more or you gonna see a side of me you won't like!" I yelled. This spawn of Satan knew how to push my buttons.

"Tuh! I don't like all the sides you got now with your round self."

"Oh you got the right one now baby! Let me tell you one thing." I started but was cut off by Gavon snatching the phone from my hand. The Lord had that boy to step in cause the cussing she was about to get would have surely landed me in the "Hellbound" line. Angels would have been using white out on my name in the Book of Life when I was done. Lord thank you for delivering me.

"Aye man! I done told you about disrespecting my grandma. You don't want these problems Chardonnay!" he yelled at her. Now I didn't like for a man to mistreat or beat a woman so instead of letting my grandson go lay hands on this jezebel I was gonna do it for him. God must've hidden my left shoe cause He wouldn't let me find it to save my life.

"Ma what you doin?" He asked focusing on me.

"Oh baby we bout to go over to this hussy's house. I'm gonna give her the beating her mammy should have given her." Where was my doggone shoe?

"Tell that old bird if she come over here she not making it back!" I heard her yell through the phone.

"Old bird? Tell her I got her old bird! Tell her them tracks she had in her head the other day looked like a bunch of old birds been pecking in it! Old bird, hmph" she done made me mad now. I was all out of Christian character I was letting the old me slip out. Jesus fix it!

"WHAT?" I heard Gavon yell. Whatever was just said seemed to drain the color from his dark handsome face. The boy was turning white in front of my eyes as he stood there.

"Baby what's wrong?" I said hobbling over to him. All that moving around looking for that shoe had done irritated my knees and now I was in pain. But the physical pain I was feeling was nothing like the emotional pain I felt with his next words.

"Chardonnay is pregnant."

Jesus take me now.

Gavon

I had no clue what Reverend Rockmore was preaching on this morning. I halfway wanted to be here after the revelation I received last night. He was speaking on something about the Prodigal son but here I was about to possibly have a son or daughter of my own.

Service seemed to drag on or maybe it just felt like that. Either way I was ready to go home. I had a lot of thinking that needed to be done. As soon as I heard the invitation to receive salvation I got up and walked outside. I needed some fresh air because it felt like everything was being sucked out of me in there and it was hard to breathe. I knew my grandma would be disappointed that I didn't wait until he gave the benediction but I would deal with that later. Besides she wasn't too fond of me at the moment.

When I told her that Chardonnay was pregnant I just knew she was about to die and that look she gave me should have taken me with her.

I stayed up for the rest of the night trying to wrap my head around this news and for the life of me I couldn't believe it. Something inside of me was telling me that wasn't my baby because I've always protected myself when I laid up with Chardonnay but there has been a few times right before I got stabbed that I didn't. But she wouldn't have known already if that baby was mine because that was only about three weeks ago that we did it. I may not have been an honor's student but I paid attention in Biology class and knew that a woman wouldn't find out she was pregnant until at least the fifth or sixth week. About a week or so after she missed her cycle.

So either Chardonnay had trapped me by putting a hole in one of the condoms or she had been fooling around on me. I was so deep into my thoughts that I didn't notice the presence of someone else until I felt their hand on my back.

"Hey handsome," Chasiti said smiling. She looked nice in her navy blue dress that had a gold belt around her waist. Her hair was pinned up in a mound of curls and her nude lipstick made her pouty lips stand out even more. The gold flats she wore went well with her gold accessories and it was something about the ankle bracelet she wore that made her already bowed legs seem longer. This girl was beautiful.

"Good morning gorgeous," I said as I hugged her. Holding her felt so right like this was where I needed to be. Just as I got comfortable in her embrace the words that my grandmother said to me came rushing back to my mind so I pulled away.

"Are you still coming over for dinner?" She asked. I saw the disappointment on her face that I had let her go.

"Naw he ain't coming! He has to take his baby's mother out for Sunday dinner," I turned to see Chardonnay standing there rubbing her stomach.

Her green and blue bob was once again a bird's nest and she had on way too much makeup. And lets not get started on the outfit she had on. I don't know what made her think coming to the house of God dressed like she had just left the stage of Magic City was ok. Standing there looking at her now really made me reevaluate what it was about her that had a hold on me.

I had always heard the warnings that Mama Jean gave about being careful who we connected with because some of these bonds could cause a world of hurt. I think she called them soul ties. Those ties could either be good for you or harm you and the bad ones were hard to let go. Some could even be to the death or as she said, be the cause of your death. That thought alone sent a chill down my spine and confirmed that if I didn't seek God to help me get rid of this girl she was gonna cause me to lose my life. Either naturally or spiritually, but never the less it would be a painful one.

"Cat got your tongue?" I heard Chardonnay say and saw the back of Chasiti as she walked back in the church. Before she walked in she turned around to look at me and I saw her wipe the fresh tear that had fallen.

Turning around I could have slapped this demon before me with this ugly smirk on her face.

"What are you doing here Chardonnay? Don't demons turn to dust once they step on holy ground?"

"Real cute. Why don't you summon your mother and ask her?" She snapped realizing she had just crossed the line. Before she could step out of reach I grabbed her by her collar.

"I promise if you ever utter another word about my mother again I will kill you." I stated through gritted teeth. The look on her face was one that surprised me. Instead of her looking afraid like I had intended she looked turned on. I let her go but not before she said, "Daddy you promise?"

I have to get away from her cause this broad was looney. She put me in the mind of this lady from round the way named Monica. Word was she left here a while back trying to get her son's father back from his wife but she ended up dead. The girl was gone even back in the day so I knew she had some mental problems. Chardonnay must have been related to her cause she was just as crazy.

"Stay away from me man," I said getting into my car and pulling off. I wasn't worried about how Mama Jean would get home because I knew she was going to the Rev's house for dinner. I just needed time to clear my head and think about what I was going to do with my life.

Chasiti

I couldn't believe that my heart ached like this. Why was I going through all of these emotions over a man that wasn't mine? Granted he didn't know how I felt about him because I never said anything but I never thought he would take a second look at me.

Walking back towards my grandfather's study I didn't realize I was still crying until Mama Jean stopped me. I loved this little old lady something serious. Papa never remarried after Granny passed before I was born so I never got a chance to know her. But Mama Jean was always there if I needed her. About a year after I came to live with Papa she was the one who sat me down to talk with me about my body and the changes I would experience. Whenever I needed her she was there and treated me just like I was her own. I adored her so much. Because of the life Gavon was living we never really hung out although I was so close to his grandma.

"Baby why you crying?" She said reaching out to me as i fell into her arms. These were the moments I cherished.

"It's nothing. Just full off of the word today," I lied. Lord forgive me.

"You better stop lying on the Holy Spirit up in His house. Your Papa can give a word but he didn't shut it down today like last Sunday." She said calling me on my bluff.

"It's just I went to go check on Gavon and while I was talking to him that ole hood rat of his popped up." I said frustrated and folding my arms across my chest. That girl irked me to no end.

Mama Jean walked over to the window looking all around."Hmph. I'm surprised she didn't turn into dust as soon as she pulled into the parking

lot. She know God don't like her." I couldn't help

but laugh.

"Mama Jean you know that's not right. I'm

sure God loves even her."

"I didn't say nothing bout Him not loving

her. I said He don't like her. You know God don't

like ugly!" By now I was too weak and so was she. I

laughed so hard until my side hurt. This woman had

just called that girl ugly and I was too tickled.

Somehow she always knew how to lift my spirit

when I was down.

"All jokes aside though. Dry those eyes and

just pray harder for him. Gavon may not understand

everything that he is feeling or going through but I

trust God in His process. In the end Gavon will

walk in his calling. And his wife will be right by his

side." She said winking at me when she said the word "wife".

For as long as I could remember I had the biggest crush on him and prayed one day God would mold him to be fit for me. That's why it was so easy for me to give him blood that night. Yeah I may have told him that's what a Christian would do but that was only the half. That's what my heart told me to do for him. Only now I wasn't so sure that if we did get together that I would be able to handle baby mama drama. I guess it was time for me to just move on and if it was meant to be then it would. I just wouldn't put my life on hold for it.

———

We made it back to Papa's house to get settled for dinner. A few of the elders in the church had come over to join us. I was the only young one in attendance but I didn't mind. I loved being around all of the wisdom that came from each of them.

I watched as Mama Jean interacted with everyone like she was the woman of the house and Papa just let her. They were so comfortable around each other that I wondered why they never married. I had never asked because they were grown but one day I would sit down and ask my grandfather. I wanted him to be happy. He deserved it and so did she. And they seemed to be happier when they were together.

The doorbell rang and I dried my hands on the dish towel.

"I got it," I said. I already knew who it was before I even opened it.

Mario stood there looking real dapper. He had been blowing me up since our first date when I left him at Lady and Sons so I finally called him back to try and make it up to him. After the episode at church I needed to clear my mind so I thought I would give him a call and invite him to dinner. That way Papa could meet him and give me his opinion later.

"Hey. I'm glad you could make it on such short notice," I said as I gave him a quick hug. His hand dipped a little low on my back and before I could say anything to him I heard someone clear their throat.

"Ahem," I heard Papa say. I knew his darn radar was going off.

"Papa this is my friend Mario. Mario this is my grandfather Reverend Mitchell Rockmore," I introduced the two.

"Good afternoon sir." Mario said reaching out his hand to shake Papa's. But Papa didn't budge.

"Be nice," I mouthed to him and only then did he stick his hand out to greet him.

"You are just in time we are about to sit down and eat," I said gently pushing my grandfather into the dining room as we walked behind him. I couldn't decipher the look on his face but it didn't look good.

"Everyone this this my friend Mario. I invited him over to enjoy dinner with us," I said introducing him to everyone. He may have had a smile on his face but I could tell he was nervous. When I followed his eyes to see what had his feet stuck to the floor and caused him to swallow hard, they landed on Mama Jean. The look on her face was that of a killer. I wondered if she was feeling some kind of way because she knew how I felt about her grandson but here I was inviting someone else over to dinner. Whatever it was I was sure she would tell me later.

Finally we sat down at the long dinner table and immediately my stomach began showing out. There was fried chicken, baked mac and cheese, collard greens with smoked neckbones, yams, BBQ ribs, baked fish, black eyes peas, corn on the cob, hot water corn bread, and two chocolate cakes for dessert. It was about to be on!

I noticed that Mama Jean and Mother West kept looking in our direction with scowls on their faces and Mario was clearly uncomfortable. Especially when Papa started grilling him. So far he was handling himself ok but I knew he was not wanting to be here much longer.

Right before dessert was served there was another knock at the door. Papa got up to get it and I heard his laughter as he greeted whoever it was at the door. It was a few seconds before he returned and he wasn't alone.

"Look who we have here," He said as I looked up and almost choked on my cake.

Gavon stood there with the ugliest look I had ever seen and it was directed straight at Mario. To my surprise Mario had the same look on his face. All I could think about was what have I gotten myself into?

Gavon

Now here I was staring this dude right in the eye. What was he even doing here? And why is he sitting next to my girl? I looked over at her and she couldn't look at me for long because she knew.

"Boy don't just stand there, come in the kitchen so I can get you something to eat." I followed Mama Jean in the kitchen.

"Listen to me and listen to me good," Mama Jean whispered. "We know that boy is up to no good. I feel it in my spirit. I want you to go out there and act like you got the sense God gave you. Don't go out there and embarrass me in front of Rev. Now Chasiti didn't know you were coming so you can't be mad at her," she shoved the plate in my hand.

"Ma I'm not even hungry."

"Boy! I swear fo Lord if you go out there and show out I'm gone slap you so hard your mama gone feel it. Do you understand me?"

"Yea. Yea I hear ya man dang," I walked out with the plate in my hand. Chasiti was no longer at the table but her male companion was. I needed to find out who this cat was because he reminded me of the same dude that keeps popping up everywhere. I made sure to sit right across from him as I stuffed my mouth. I looked at his right hand that had a bullet tattooed on it, I looked up at him and he had this smirk on his face. I mugged him back and finished my food as I listened to the old folks talk about church. Chasiti never returned, so I excused myself from the table to go and see where she was. I'd never been in Rev. house before but I wanted to see what was up, I hope I wasn't falling for someone that already had somebody.

When I found her she was in the backyard sitting on the swing under a big oak tree. When I walked up it sounded like she was praying so I didn't move until I thought she was finished. I couldn't make everything out that she was saying but I heard my name several times as I approached her.

"Why did you run off?" I asked after I heard her say amen.

"Don't do that. You scared me," she grabbed her chest.

"I'm sorry," we both laughed. Chasiti was so cute to me, she made me feel like I was wanted and needed when I was around her.

"Gavon I apologize for inviting Mario over. You left without telling me anything so I didn't want to be here alone."

"It's cool. So how long you been knowing…what's his face in there?"

"His name is Mario, Gavon. He's a nice dude. We went out once."

"So what do you know about him," I tried picking her brain.

"I mean I don't know much this is only our second time seeing each other," Chasiti explained.

"So you don't know nothing about him. Is that what you telling me?"

"Gavon you don't know him either. If you follow me back in the house I'll introduce you to him if it's such a big deal."

"Nah we good on that. I don't want to meet him at all," I gave her a little attitude.

I pushed her on the swing until we were interrupted by her date.

"Untmmm," he cleared his throat behind us. "Am I interrupting something?" he asked.

"Yea I'm out here having a private conversation and here you go," I looked him in his face. Mama Jean always told me to look a man in the eye and how the eyes told a story. Looking at this cat he didn't have much of a story to tell. He didn't have that same look that my uncle them had, now those was some real g's if I ever seen any.

"I'm sorry for leaving you in there so long. I just needed some fresh air. By the way Mario this is my friend Gavon, Gavon this is Mario," Chasiti introduced us.

"Nice to meet you," he held his hand out. I mugged him and walked back towards the house. I was ready to go and I was hoping Mama Jean was ready by now.

"Ma you ready?" I asked her as she was cackling at the table.

She gave me a menacing look, "Don't you see me talking boy? Now get out my face."

I knew better than to ask her was she ready once I seen her talking to Rev. Rockmore about church. Mama Jean done slapped me in my mouth several times for talking while she was in the middle of a conversation. Mama Jean still had it if you caught her right, she would look at you with those beady eyes and talk through her teeth, you better move out her way. I went and waited in the car and listened to Solo Lucci on my iPod. I could really use a blunt right now but I wasn't gone light up in my grandma's car. Today had really been a disaster, I thought Chardonnay popping up at church was bad but coming over here to spend some time with Chasiti and here's Mario over here sitting next to her eating dinner like he's part of the family.

Right as that cat crossed my mind, Chasiti came walking him to his car. Mario was getting to the money driving this brand new Benz. You didn't see too many folks riding like that in Savannah, I had my eye on him. All the while Chasiti was talking to him he kept his face in his phone, I wonder who he was texting so much. Chasiti waved as he backed up, when he looked up to see me grilling him, he put his middle finger at me. I gave him a gun symbol just to let him know I was coming for his head.

"Gavon!" Chasiti hit my window to get my attention. I unlocked the door to let her in.

"You good?"

"Yea I'm real good," I glanced up the road at Mario's taillights as I started my grandma's car and headed in the other direction.

Chasiti

"Chasiti do you mind taking an ole lady home?" Mama Jean asked me after we finished the dishes.

"Of course not. Let me go and get my stuff together and I'll be ready."

I walked in my old room to gather my purse and cell phone charger before entering back in the living room to my Papa giving Mama Jean a hug goodnight. Both of them were so lonely and I don't think they would make it if they didn't have Gavon and I.

"I'm ready. Papa I'll text you when I get home." I tiptoed to kiss him on the cheek and I helped Mama Jean down the three stairs and to my car.

"Chasiti you know you are such a wonderful girl. Why you ain't got no man yet?"

I laughed because Mama Jean was so blunt it almost made you think she was still young with how she talked to you.

"Mama Jean I haven't found a man that walks upright. I mean I'm a lot of woman. I have a great deal of responsibility and I don't want to just settle for a man. I've done that in the past and I jeopardized my Christianity to be with that man. Right now the only thing right in my life is Jesus. These men out here still running the streets, they not worried about God or where their soul is going to rest when it's all over."

"You so right baby. I try to tell Gavon the streets don't love him, these same streets gone bring him back to me in a body bag. You pray for my baby because he wants to do right but that old devil got a good hold on him. I know the Lord gone bring about a change in him, I just pray it's before I leave here. I would love to see it and experience it with Gavon."

"You will Mama Jean, I'll be praying with you."

We pulled up to Mama Jean's driveway and I got out to help her in the house, but before I could get far Gavon was coming out without a shirt on to help her inside. I swallowed hard and got back in my car and locked the door saying a quick prayer.

That was the last thing I needed to see was a man I like without his shirt on. He flicked the light on the porch to let me know they made it in the house and closed the door. Once I got myself together I sped off heading home and trying to get Gavon off my brain.

"Lord I don't ask for much. But ask that you shape Gavon into the man of God he supposed to be. I see his potential but God I ask that you show it to him as well. Change his heart for the streets and turn it to you. The things he has planned that are not in your will, make them impossible. That's all I ask in Jesus name Amen."

I pulled the cover back and climbed in bed. I was tired from all of today's events, I wanted to know what the issue was between Gavon and Mario. I didn't want to be in the middle of a war and surely I didn't want it to be because of me. If I had to leave someone alone it would be Mario, I didn't know him enough to lose Gavon and my relationship with Mama Jean. There was something off about Mario, he was always on his phone texting. The whole time I was talking to him tonight he was on his phone. Maybe I needed to find out what he does for a living and that would tell me why he was on the phone. The thing I loved about Gavon, when I was around he gave me all of his attention.

I rolled over to grab my phone and send him some encouraging words. I know he was stressed about the whole baby thing. Even with Chardonnay in the picture it didn't change how I felt about Gavon. What girl from around the way didn't use that "I'm pregnant" line when a man don't want them no more? I deeply wanted to show Chardonnay she wasn't as bad as she portrayed to be but I refused to lower my standards, bedsides we all know she lies just like she did at the hospital which caused me to get suspended and almost lose my job.

I smiled when he texted back "thank you and goodnight" I put my phone back on the nightstand and drifted off to sleep.

Mama Jean

Boy I tell you the truth if I didn't love this nappy headed grandson of mine he would've been out my house. Here it was 2 something in the afternoon and he was laying up here in this room still sleep with his mouth wide open and dreads all over the place. And his room smelled like he was growing weed right here in the house.

"I should shove my dirty knee high in his mouth," I said before hitting him in the chest with my open hand.

"Whaa…What you do that for Ma?" he wiped his eyes.

"Gavon do you have any idea what time it is? If you don't get out this bed and look at your eyes, that's why you can't get up because you a pot head. Let me find out you dipping into some other drugs, I'm gone drag you right into the middle if the hood and drop you off with your no good uncles now play if you want to. NOW GET UP!" I slapped his door so hard I heard my wrist pop. He had me so worked up my stomach was burning from my ulcer. I took my time going back down the stairs. It didn't take long before Gavon had showered and came downstairs and ask what need to be done.

"Sit down Gavon," I pointed over at the rocking chair on the side of me. I was enjoying the nice fall season that was slowly creeping in.

"Yes ma'am?"

"Gavon what do you plan on doing with your life? I'm not gone live forever you do know that right. I think I've done okay with raising you without your parents, but it's time to get serious about your life. What do you plan on doing about this Chardonnay girl? Now she done popped up talking about she pregnant."

"Mama Jean you don't have to worry about that. If she is it's not mine, you know that girl will go to extreme measures to be with me. I mean I plan to move you out the hood and be rich and open some businesses."

"You sound ignorant you know that. You been laying up with that girl. I can't deny that the girl ain't crazy, sometimes I believe I'm gone have to put my hands on her before it's all over. And me moving out of my house is not gone happen so don't even think about it. All I'm saying is you need to try to connect with people that's gone push you towards something great. Now my Chasiti baby will be the one to help you become a better man," I looked over at him.

"From the looks of it she's occupied with that Mario dude."

"Boy please. Mario can't do nothing with Chasiti. Mario look like he came straight from Planet of the Apes with all them golds in his mouth. Who comes to Rev. house looking like a thug, he would never make it. You don't have to worry about him too much longer. And tell me how you plan on getting rich without an education or job."

"Ma just know we gone be good. Now what needs to be done around the house before I head out for the day?"

"Boy I did everything as long as you laid up there in that bed. I may need you to go get some groceries that's about it. I'm going to see your daddy this week. I would love for you to come with me, you've been on his list for years and you never go."

"Not today ma okay. I don't want to talk about it, can you just respect that for the moment. I'm not trying to be disrespectful but I don't want to talk about that man right now. I got enough going on and he only makes things worse."

I put my hands up and started back rocking in my chair as Gavon walked back in the house. I had a stack of letters I need Gavon to read, I knew his heart wasn't ready so I kept them when they came in the mail. I made Alvin aware of it so he wouldn't be in prison wondering had Gavon read the letters. If Gavon would grow up he would know the truth. I wasn't gone force it, but every now and then I was gone mention his daddy. Gavon had the mentality that people live forever but that was far from the truth. I didn't want to leave here and my grandson not know the truth about his father and mother.

Alvin

I had another dream about my wife. She was the most gorgeous woman I've ever seen, I knew when I met her I had to make her my wife. Everyone told me I was moving too fast because she was a hood chick and I was just another dude from around the way that was raised up in the struggle. After wining and dining her for about three months, we were married and pregnant with Gavon. I was finally happy with my life and would work three jobs just to make sure they were happy. I knew Mama Jean was coming to see me soon but I felt the need to write my son this letter. I didn't know how much time I was gone be able to hold on, I didn't have my wife and my son didn't want me in his life. That was my whole life before I got placed in the cage.

I put my pen to paper and wrote my son possibly what would be my last letter. The tears started falling on the page and I could hardly see because the tears were blocking my vision. I needed a miracle from God because my heart was hurting something serious. I prayed every night for my son, God had yet to deliver. I just wanted to see him, hug and make sure he had everything he needed on the outside world. I didn't want the streets raising my son. The streets claimed his mama and blamed me for it, I depleted all my resources trying to get my case opened back up and I couldn't ask Mama Jean for anything because she's done more than enough.

I wrapped the letter up with telling him how much I love him before I folded it up and put it in the envelope and sat it on the little desk before getting on my knees. I didn't have any words for God today, I couldn't cry anymore and I couldn't think of words to say. I intertwined my hands together and closed my eyes and just hoped that God could understand my heart and my silence. I stayed down there until my knees started hurting. It was just about time for me to get my hour outside so as usual I'll take my quick run and do my exercises. I been down all these years but I kept my body just like my wife liked it. I walked over to my little desk and pick the small picture up with her on it and rubbed my hand over her face. *God please come through for me.*

Chardonnay

I popped my gum as I looked at Mario showing up to my house. I hadn't seen him since he went to Chasiti's granddaddy house for Sunday dinner and here he was like he don't know why I got an attitude. Since Gavon broke it off with me, money slowed down just a tad. I had plenty of people to pay my way but Gavon's money took care of my personal needs like my hair, nails and clothes. Gee may not have been getting big paper out in these streets but what he did get he gave to me. So I needed Mario to come through with some coins today. I smacked my lips and rolled my eyes at him. I sat and waited on him to say something but he never did so that took me over the edge.

"So where you been for three days Mario?"

"Chardonnay don't start that nagging now dang. I'm tired and I don't feel like being bothered, I came over here to go to the doctor with you that's it."

"So that's it?"

"Yea that baby in your stomach is my only concern."

"Wow," I got up off my sofa and went and got my purse and walked out the door leaving him in the living room. After making me wait for ten minutes he finally came out of the house on his phone. He ticked me off always on that phone. I think I made a huge mistake putting him on this job. After my doctor's appointment he did take me to get something to eat and was ready to drop me off but I wasn't having it.

"You not coming in?"

"Nah," he said without looking at me.

"Why?"

"Look Char I don't think this thing between us gone work. I'm gone take care of the baby but me and you, we done. You make me put my hands on you and I don't like that."

Before I realized it I was sitting there crying my eyes out and he didn't care one bit. I tried to touch him and he snatched away. Oh I see what this was about to be. I got myself together before my lashes came off and I really started looking a mess. I didn't have the money to get them redone if they did.

"You falling for her huh?" I asked him.

"I mean she different, something I'm not use too. So I want to spend some more time with her to see how things go and I ask that you respect that." He said calmly like we didn't have a plan in place.

"I know what you're thinking and I'm not going through with it. My issue is with homeboy not her and I don't want her to get involved." He was serious and I knew that I would have to remove her myself. So I let him have this at the moment. She would get hers one way or another.

I just looked at him in silence before he hit the unlock button on the doors and I knew that was my que to get out. I had to figure out what was up with this Chasiti chick and why she was pulling all my men. I didn't expect Mario to fall for her, she wasn't his type. Mario was a real hood boy with the golds in his mouth, chains around his neck and a wad of cash in his pocket. Today he was not that Mario, he was dressed up with a pair of jeans and collar shirt and he didn't have his golds in his mouth. I pulled the door handle to let myself out. I stood on my doorstep as he pulled off probably heading to see Chasiti. I reached in my purse and grabbed my keys to my car making sure to give Mario enough time to make it to the first stop light before I started following him. I was at least five cars behind him when he got off on the first exit, I slowed down so he wouldn't notice me getting off the exit with him. He mashed the brakes and it startled me so I pulled over and let another car go ahead of me. He turned down a one way street into a little neighborhood so I waited at the gas station to give him time to make it to her house.   Once I thought he was in her house good enough I started driving down the neighborhood real slow until I seen his car. By the time I got down the street he was pulling off with Chasiti in the car, I pulled in a driveway so fast so he wouldn't catch me. See now I was heated, he was just at my house and went to the doctor with me and now here he was coming to pick her up for a date I was assuming. I couldn't continue to chase them because my cover would be blown. Maybe my plan worked after all and I can get Gavon back. Mario may have thought he was no longer helping me but in a way he was. I smiled before backing out of the stranger's house and riding down to see what little Ms. Chasiti's address was.

"Gavon yo' lil rat out here," I heard Mama Jean say before I got out the car.

I swear if I could get away with it I would get rid of her and sit at her funeral like I don't know what happened. I walked up to the porch where she sitting drinking her sweet tea and shucking peas.

"Hey Mama Jean," I said dryly.

"So I heard you pregnant huh," she looked at me over her glasses.

"Yes ma'am."

"When you due? You look a good ways. When your next appointment so I can be there. If you gone bring my great grandchild in the world I want to be there every step of the way." She fired off at me.

"I actually just left. I'm sorry I didn't know you wanted to go, I'll make sure you are aware of the next appointment."

"So you mean to tell me you walked out the doctor office without an appointment card? I got three kids and way back then we didn't have them new school doctors yall go to now. But when my daughter had Gavon she never left without them giving her another appointment before she left."

"No my doctor wasn't in today so I saw the nurse," I lied quickly. I wasn't expecting Gavon to tell his grandma this quick about the pregnancy. I was in a mess because Mama Jean was pesky and she didn't give up on nothing until she got the answer she needed.

"What you want Chardonnay?" Gavon came out with his dreads hanging over his shoulder.

"I wanted to talk to you about the baby," I pleaded with my eyes.

Come on," he waved for me to come in the house. Mama Jean eyed me as I walked past her and into the house.

"I wanted to tell you I went to the doctor today and everything is looking good," I smiled at him as I sat on his bed.

"Chardonnay let's be real. We both know that baby ain't mine so why you even playing. I'm not dumb, I haven't sleep with you in a minute. So whose baby is it? Is it that cat you was twerking on at the club?"

"No this is your baby Gee I promise. And why are you over here stressing about somebody I was twerking on months ago. You need to be worried about why your new fling going out on dates with a new dude." I smiled after I felt like my seed was sown. I noticed a change in his attitude which was all I wanted.

Without another word I got up and walked out of the house to my car. I didn't even bother saying goodbye to him or his grandma.

Mario

Chardonnay was so dumb. She thought I didn't see her crazy behind following me, she's the only one with all of that pink mess in her car. The car even had those old ugly eyelashes on the headlights. She was crazy but she didn't want to go there with me. I wasn't Gavon and I didn't mind putting her in her place, she knew she didn't want Chasiti to know we knew each other. If Chasiti had any inclination of us she would know that we were plotting on her and Gavon. Now that I was feeling her I didn't want her find out at all. I was gonna have to pay Chardonnay a little visit. In the meantime I would definitely enjoy this time with Chasiti and get to know her a little better.

"So where are you taking me?" she asked me with that beautiful smile of hers.

"I thought maybe we would catch a movie and then go and eat dinner. I talked with your grandfather already and he knows where you are," I reassured her.

"Wait you did what? Now that's a first. My Papa don't like nobody since my last break up," She sounded shocked.

"Well I'm not your last breakup. Let's just get to know each other a little better," I said as I set my eyes back on the road.

We enjoyed the movie together. I even softened up and went to see a chick flick with her. We ended up at the Huddle House because she had a taste for waffles. I wasn't too fond of taking her to the hood but it was what she wanted. I made sure to take her to one that I knew nothing was gone come bite me in the butt. I was deep in these streets and the last thing I wanted or needed was for someone that knew me and what I did to run into me while we were together.

We enjoyed casual conversation and I enjoyed being around her but I had a feeling in my gut it would be short lived.

"Mario, what's up homeboy? I was just talking to my cousin about you. He was looking for a lick and I told him you were the one to see bout that," he laughed showing his golds.

I just sat there and stared at him with no response hoping he would catch the drift. I could see the look of confusion on Chasiti's face and I hoped she didn't ask what was going on.

"My bad homie, I see you on a date. I'll holler at you round the way." He dapped me up and walked off to order his food.

After he walked away I looked over at Chasiti, and she seemed unbothered about the whole conversation now I knew she wasn't dumb so I knew she picked up on the conversation. I just hoped she didn't start asking any questions. I wasn't gone stress the issue though, it was getting late and I still needed to see Chardonnay before I headed home. I dropped Chasiti off and headed right to the middle of the hood.

"Chardonnay open up the door right now!" I beat on the door.

"Why you beating on my door this late?" I snatched Chardonnay up by her neck and slammed her up on the wall and got in her grill.

"So you call yourself following me today huh? Next time you try to be slick try it with someone that ain't from the streets like your little flunky Gavon. Chardonnay you know not to play with me like that. Now stay in your lane, if I see you again it's not gone be pretty." I let her neck go and watched as she held on to her neck and started crying.

I got in my car and headed to my house. I was disgusted with Chardonnay, I was the type of dude to always have a thing for a good hood chick. Chardonnay was my type until Chasiti came in the picture. This girl had me from the first date that she walked out on, I knew I was ready for something fresh. I knew she wasn't gonna be easy. Church girls tried to put on a front like they were all goody two shoes but I knew better. Chasiti had a soft spot for me I could tell and it wouldn't be long before I had her all to myself.

I stripped out of my clothes and grabbed my black n mild and turned on my big screen. If I could get Chasiti to fall for a thug like me I would give her the world, I could see her now walking around my big house and cooking and cleaning and helping me raise my little one. There was no way I was gone let Chardonnay raise my child, she couldn't take care of herself the way she been looking lately. Chasiti was a little on the thick side but that was something I was willing to get used to just to be with her.

Chasiti

I got out of the shower thinking about the evening that I just experienced. When Mario called me and asked if he could take me out I really didn't want to go. But I knew in order to get the answers that I needed I had to play along so I let him. Every time he looked at me I would smile just because I wanted to be nice but not because I was glad that I was in his presence. Mario wasn't to be trusted and I knew that there was something up.

He didn't know it but I saw Chardonnay's car when he came to pick me up. This dummy had made it so obvious as she swerved into the Parker's driveway trying to go unnoticed. I knew Mario saw her because he tensed up and tried to smile it off. How could anyone not notice that ratchet thing she called a car. She was the only one in Savannah that had those dang lashes on her lights and the inside looked like a bottle of Pepto Bismol had exploded. And there was one thing that we did in my neighborhood, we actually knew who our neighbors were. Chardonnay stuck out like a sore thumb and she didn't even realize it.

Mario tried to make me feel comfortable and probably under different circumstances I would have. Maybe even falling some for him but it just wasn't in my heart. For as long as I could remember I had a crush on Gavon from afar and I felt like this was the timing that God had appointed for us to be together. I knew it wouldn't be easy but in the end it would be worth it.

I scrolled down my timeline on Facebook looking at all of the posts from the Saints and Aint's. This was entertainment that I didn't have to leave my house to get. There was someone always in their feelings about something. Nothing was going on too much so I decided to log off for the night. I didn't have to work the next day thanks to Chardonnay so I lay in bed with nothing but Gavon on my mind.

Not too long after I finally dozed off I heard my phone notify me of a message. I opened it and instantly got an attitude.

Mario: U sleep?

Me: Yea

Mario: You dreaming about me?

Me: I bet you would like that wouldn't you?

Ugh he was so cocky and I couldn't stand that about him but I had to play along. I knew there was something that was going on with him and I had a feeling deep in my spirit that it had a lot to do with Gavon. So until I found out I would have to keep up this façade.

Mario: I'd like to be there with u. I'll let you go tho.

Me: Ok. Goodnight.

That was the end of that conversation. I don't know what Mario thought but I wasn't an easy one to get to. I put my phone back on my nightstand and before I could get comfortable my doorbell rang.

"I know good and well this man did not pop up at my house!" I fumed. I got out of the bed and walked to the door with an attitude. If Papa knew I didn't ask who it was before I opened the door he would have a heart attack. Whoever it was they were about to meet "Chat" my ghetto alter ego.

Swinging the door open I almost passed out to see Gavon standing there like he had the weight of the world on his shoulders.

"Hey." I said. Lord this man did something to me that I couldn't explain and I knew I would have to repent later.

"I'm sorry to come by so late. I tried calling first but when you didn't answer I got worried." He said.

"Oh I was asleep. When I got back from my date with Mario I was tired." I honestly told him. I saw the look on his face and knew the mention of Mario's name did something to him.

"Well since you're ok I'll holla at you." He said as he turned to walk away.

"Wait. You don't have to leave." I know that had to be the little devil sitting on my shoulder that said that.

"You sure. It's pretty late." He said with a look of hope on his face.

"Yeah." The little devil answered as she unlocked the screen door. Where was the angel when I needed her?

He came in, closed the door, and locked it behind him. I walked over to the couch and turned on the television and lamp that was on the table. I knew that something was bothering him but I didn't want to pry. I also wanted to tell him what I was feeling and the real reason that I was hanging with Mario but I didn't want to jump the gun and start something that wasn't there. Gavon was a hot head and I could tell that Mario was as well. The last thing that I wanted to do was start a war between the two with no facts. So I would remain quiet.

I watched Gavon as he walked around the living room looking at the many pictures on my mantle and walls. Most were of me and Papa and a few were of my parents. When he got to the one of my mother and I he picked it up and stared at it.

"You look just like her." He said smiling. I got up and walked over to where he was standing and took the picture out of his hand and looked at it before placing it back on the shelf.

I felt his hand touch my face and that's when I realized that I was crying. It amazed me how vulnerable I was able to be around him and it didn't make me uncomfortable. This was one of the reasons that I never sat in this room because of all of the memories. They were so painful and still felt so fresh.

"I wish she loved me as much as she loved everything else." I said breaking the silence between us.

He didn't say anything in response. All he did was wipe the fresh fallen tears and lead me over to the couch. Sitting with his back facing the arm of the chair he kicked his shoes off and put his leg up on the couch. I wasn't sure if this was a good idea but I allowed him to pull me down between his legs as he laid my head back on his chest. I closed my eyes once he started rubbing his fingers through my hair and that's when I remembered I looked a mess. I was so mad that I thought Mario was popping up to my house that I didn't even take the time to brush my hair.

Gavon must have felt me tense up and he chuckled. "Yeah your hair was standing up on your head like some chickens had been fighting in it."

"Shut up Gee!" I laughed.

A few more minutes passed before he spoke again.

"Do you think that you could forgive her?" he asked me.

I was lost at first because I had forgotten we were just talking about my mother.

"I already have," was my simple reply. I told him how my childhood was all the way up until Papa came to get me at the age of ten. From the days where her and my father would be so high that they couldn't even make sure that I was fed or made it to school. To the days where they stayed in their room so long I thought they were dead. Papa tried so hard and long to get them to give their lives over to the Lord but they just refused. The final showdown came when Papa showed up one day to pick me up for the weekend and he caught my mother getting ready to let my father and his friend take advantage of me. I had burn marks on my arms and legs from where they would put their cigarettes out on my skin. I hadn't eaten since the last time Papa had dropped me off. They had been so far gone that this time they forgot that he was coming this weekend. Normally they would have everything looking to be in order by the time he got there. I knew I could tell Papa but I was scared that they would keep me from seeing him if I did. His house was the only place that I had peace. There and church of course.

I explained how he got there right before they pumped my little body with the drugs they had in the syringe and the man was able to violate me. By the time I finished telling my story I had completely broken down and cried uncontrollably. I don't know why I felt shame and that Gavon would look at me any differently but sometimes that's how certain situations we went through made us feel.

He was quiet as he held me close to his chest and just let me cry. I didn't realize that after all of these years I was still a little bitter on the inside towards my parents. I wanted so bad to not hold on to this stuff in my heart, that I just pretended that everything was ok. It was crazy how this man sitting with me was able to bring all of these different emotions out of me whenever he was around. God what is going on?

Gavon

I don't know what made me come over to this girl's house this late without calling but I felt like I was about to lose my mind. All of these emotions about what happened to me, the state of Chardonnany and I, Chasiti entertaining this new cat, and most of all the relationship with my father Mama Jean was adamant I needed to fix. I didn't feel like I owed him nothing. If it wasn't for him my mother would still be alive. It was just so much to handle as I rode the streets of Savannah and before I knew it I was ringing Chasiti's doorbell.

"I didn't mean to come over here and upset you." I told her as I continued to hold her. It just felt so right being with her and being able to comfort her. After hearing her story I had a deeper admiration for her because of what she went through at such a young age. She went through so much but that only made her work harder to come out of it. And she still trusted God. I guess that's what stuck out to me the most.

"No it's not your fault. I guess you were heaven sent because I needed to release that. I haven't talked to anyone about my childhood but Papa and Mama Jean." She said shocking me. I knew her and my grandmother had a really good relationship but I didn't know that it was this deep.

"So you talk to mama a lot huh?" I asked her.

"Yeah. She helps me with so much that Papa may not understand. Woman stuff you know?" she said rubbing her hands on her night pants and snuggling a little closer to me.

We sat a little while longer in silence. Thinking about our own lives and how we ended up where we were I guess. I was scared of the answer that I might receive but this thought had been nagging at me since Sunday dinner.

"Yo what's up with you and that Mario cat? You feeling him like that?" I asked feeling myself getting a little heated.

Chasiti turned around with this big goofy smile on her face that instantly made me forget about being mad.

"Let me find out you jealous," she said still smiling. I couldn't help feeling all warm inside looking at her and that dimple of her's.

"Maannn go 'head. Ain't nobody jealous," I tried to lie but the truth was every time I thought about her being with someone else I got mad. I knew she wasn't sleeping with anyone until marriage and I guess that's what made me desire her even more. Some days I thought about getting all the way right so that I could be that man of God that she needed but these streets kept calling me. It was like the devil was using the streets to pull me to him and then God was using Chasiti to pull me closer to Him. This tug-of-war with my life was beginning to drain me. I just wasn't sure of when I was going to give in and to what side.

I had been so deep in thought that I hadn't noticed that she was still looking me in my eyes so intently. This was one of the most beautiful women I had ever seen besides my mother and my grandma and before I knew it my lips landed on hers. I thought she would pull away from me but to my surprise she didn't and her passion matched mine. Knowing that I didn't want to put her in a compromising situation I pulled back.

"Jesus," she said just above a whisper.

"I'm sorry. I just couldn't help myself." I told her as I removed a stray curl from her face.

"What brought you over here?" she said laying her head back on my chest like what we just experienced didn't have her heart pounding. I could feel it when I had my arms around her. Thinking about what she had just asked me brought me back to the real reason I was here.

Knowing that she had just opened herself up to me I knew that I could trust her to listen to me. I motioned for her to sit up so that I could reach into my back pocket. I held on to the envelopes before I handed them to her. I watched her as she sorted through the unopened mail addressed to me.

"Who is Alvin Cunningham?" she asked looking up at me.

"My father."

"Why haven't you opened them? These go back almost twenty two years."

My father had been sending Mama Jean letters for me since I was two years old and here I am going on twenty five. My heart was so hard towards this man that she knew that I wasn't going to do anything but throw them away if I saw them so she held on to every letter that he ever mailed to me. When she received the last one today she felt like something wasn't right and that I needed to put my pride aside and read them. Instead of me listening to her I rode around with the letters in my back pocket until I ended up here with Chasity.

"I guess I'm scared to know the truth. I mean I already know it I'm just scared to hear it from him."

"Are you sure you know the truth Gee?" the way she said my name calmed me every time that I felt like snapping.

"He killed my mother. I saw him covered in blood when I was two and my mother had a gunshot wound to her head." I said as I felt my throat tightening up. I haven't cried about this since I was a little boy and I didn't want to do it tonight.

"Babe, you were just a little boy. Maybe what you saw wasn't really what happened. You were so young and could have misunderstood what it was that you saw that night." She said putting her hands through my dreads.

No one has ever explained it to me like that. I had spent all of these years hearing people tell me that I should just listen to my father and hear him out, but not why I should listen. Hearing Chasiti explain it like this changed my mind.

"Will you read them with me?" I asked her. If it was anyone I wanted to go through this with it was her. No matter what was said in these letters I knew that she would help me to get through it.

"Of course I will. And if you want me to give you some privacy then I will do that too." She said wiping the corner of my eye. I kissed her softly on her lips and opened the door I had been so scared to walk through all of these years as we began to read the first letter.

Chardonnay

It was going on three in the morning and my man was laid up in the next broad's crib. For the life of me I couldn't figure out what Chasiti had over me. I was finer than she was, I kept my hair laid, my body was banging, and I was just that fly chick. Granted I didn't have my own job or could provide for myself but I didn't have to when the men that I choose did that for me. Whatever it was she wouldn't have either of them long after what I had planned for her.

I was gathering all of the info that I needed on her and once I was able to get Mario back on my side then I knew we could use it to get her out of the picture. I had been sitting in my cousin's car down the block from her house since Gavon got over here. I had saw him driving as I was coming back from one of my little boo's houses and I followed to see where he was going. I followed him for a while and I was glad that I wasn't in my own car. He knew what it looked like even in the dark and he would have pulled over and caused a scene. I wasn't on that arguing tonight because I wanted to know what he was up to.

At first it looked like he was heading towards his grandma's house but as he passed the street that he should have turned on it piqued my interest. I was just about to give up until I realized the location we were headed in. He was headed to her house. I watched as he got out looking like he had a lot on his mind and I knew that he came here to talk to her. Gavon never talked to me about important stuff that was going on in his life and it made me wonder even more why he trusted her so much.

I watched as she swung the door open but when she saw who it was her face softened. The look on her face let me know that she had genuine love for him. Something that I didn't and it made me madder. She was the total opposite of me and that's what he needed. But I would be dead in my grave before I let that happen. As that thought came to my mind I felt a chill come over my body and nothing but goose bumps popped up on my arms.

Brushing off that eerie feeling, I took out my phone and snapped a picture of Gavon's car sitting outside of Chasiti's house and text it to Mario's phone. It wasn't long before my phone was ringing and Mario's face was showing on my screen.

"Helloooo" I sang into the receiver.

"Chardonnay what are you doing? I told you to leave this alone. Let it go!" he yelled into the phone.

"So you mad at me but yo' girl over here with the next dude in her crib in the middle of the night. You know the only thing opened this time of night is the club or legs."

"You would know huh?" he said being funny.

"Real cute Mario. Real cute." I said popping my lips.

"How I know this is even right now? You could have been had this pic and it's not even that late at night." He said trying to convince himself that I was lying. He must have really been feeling her because if it was me he wouldn't care if someone was lying on me or not. He would just believe them. That made me mad even more.

Without another word I hung up on him, stepped out of the car, and took a selfie with the car and house behind me and sent it to his phone. I didn't think the text had sent before I was receiving one back from him that simply said,

Baby Daddy: I'M ON MY WAY!

I looked down once I heard the notification of a text go off on my phone. My cheeks started to hurt as I saw the message flash across the screen.

Gavon

I grabbed the first letter dated back when I was two, from the looks of it they hadn't sent him off to prison yet because the address was different than the rest of the envelopes. Once I opened it, it was thinner than the rest of the letters too. As I unfolded the letter I tried to stop the tears from falling down my face. I tried to man up because I was around Chasiti, I didn't want her thinking I was soft. Chasiti softly took the letter out of my hand and started reading it out loud.

To my baby boy Gavon:

I know that you are still young and don't understand what's going on right now. But all I do want you to know is that daddy loves you and mommy too. She was the love of my life and if I could take her place I would. Mama Jean is going to take good care of you.

Love,

Daddy

Chasiti placed the letter on her table and wiped my tears that I never knew were falling.

"Gee I believe the more we continue to read the more you will find out about your father. From the looks of it he really loved you. And I pray that God opens your heart."

A knock on the door stopped me from responding to what she said.

"Now who in the world is this?" Chasiti walked towards the door. I got up and followed behind her to see who it was as well. I don't think neither of us were prepared for who was on the other side of the door.

"Mario what are you doing here?" Chasiti asked while looking over his shoulder.

"I just texted you maybe an hour ago and you told me you were sleep. But from the looks of it you don't look sleep," Mario crossed his arms and rubbed his chin.

"Hold on, we are not a couple. And I don't have to answer to you or anyone else." I got closer to Chasiti so Mario can see me.

"Is there a problem Chas?"

"No I'm good."

"Yea its problem little buddy," Mario said mugging me.

I pushed Chasiti out the way so I could get out the door and closer to Mario. We were now face to face nose to nose staring each other down.

"What the problem is then patna?"

Mario pushed me back into the house which caused me to knock Chasiti over in the door frame of her house.

"Move Chas!" I yelled at her once I seen Mario charging towards me. I didn't know what the beef was with us. I knew this went further than Chasiti, this dude had a real hatred for me. I got up on my feet just in time to connect my fist in Mario's stomach. We went blow for blow breaking all Chasiti's stuff, I could hear her screaming in the background. I heard another voice enter into the house that made my skin crawl.

"Get him Mario!!! I mean you better beat his behind," Chardonnay was hollering in the background.

Chasiti was a little bit stronger than I thought as she was finally able to pull me off Mario because I was a little winded from smoking all that weed. I lips were bleeding and I was sweating profusely, the shirt I came over here in was now ripped and a piece of it was across the room. Chardonnay was holding Mario and smiling at me.

"So this how you doing now Char?" I asked her.

"This how you doing it Gee," she pointed towards Chasiti.

"You know what I'm bout sick of this chick Gavon. You at my house now so it won't be nothing to beat your behind and go get right in my bed like I haven't did a thing. Now tell me what you want to do, cause you've really pushed me to my limit. And you had the nerve to bring Mario over here. This got your messy name all over it."

"Calm down Chas I got this," I moved her.

"You better get your baby mama then."

"Wait who baby?" Mario asked. "So that's what you told this dude? So who baby is it Chardonnay?" Mario stared at her.

"Yea who baby is it since you instigating mess," Chasiti said.

I looked at Chardonnay with disgust. This broad pulled the ultimate hood chick card by lying to me about a baby. I knew I wasn't the daddy but she had me second guessing myself. Her smiled wiped off her face quick once she was put on the spot.

"Cat got your tongue?" Mario looked at her. After all that fighting now the focus was on Chardonnay the person that started all this mess in first.

"Mario can we talk about this somewhere else," she looked at Chasiti.

"Nah you need to talk about this here. You just walked up to my grandfather's church breaking the news to Gavon and I about you being pregnant, now you want to talk in private. Seems to me that you playing games," Chasiti said.

"Oh you got some explaining to do Chardonnay," Mario said.

"Alright Mario it's your baby. I wanted to use Gavon too. There you happy now. Gavon you a punk and you not made for the streets. It was easy setting you up, you do the same thing every time you come over. All you were was my trick. I wish Mario would have killed you that night." "What you just said?" I was fuming now. I ripped the rest of my shirt off and squared up with Mario again. I knew he was the one that stabbed me that night. He was the same dude that was with Chardonnay at the club that night also. We went for round two right in the front yard while Chardonnay was arguing with Chasiti.

I guess we made such a fuss that the neighbors called the police on us. Mario, Chardonnay and I were both cuffed and took down to the county. The last thing I wanted was to call

Mama Jean and wake her up out of her sleep and tell her I was locked up.

Mama Jean

"Lord I'm tired of this phone ringing all times of the night." I moaned just a little as I rolled over to turn my little lamp on so I can grab the phone. Gavon was gone catch my wrath, I don't know why he won't tell this little girl to call his cell phone.

"Mama Jean," Chasiti yelled in the phone.

"Girl calm down what's wrong?"

"I'm on the way. Gavon was taken to jail."

"Baby what you just say? Lord let me get up, hurry up and come get me. I can't leave my baby in there, unt uh he can't stay in there." I slammed the phone down and sat up on the side of the bed to warm my knee up. I rubbed on it a little before I rocked to get up off the bed. I changed out of my old gown and put on my favorite moo moo and my shoes. I made sure to grab any paperwork they may need for bail.

Chasiti pulled up a few minutes later and I was sitting outside rocking in a rocking chair waiting on her with my old black purse I kept all my paperwork in.

"What happened? Why my grandbaby locked up?"

"He came over and we were talking, then Mario popped up talking trash and then something told me to pay attention and there was Chardonnay egging them on."

"See," I sad shaking my finger at no one in particular. "That little guh will make you do some things to her that only God could forgive you for. What that girl crazy do that for. So she messing with your other male friend too? What his name Marco? Mark?"

"Mario, Mama Jean."

"Yea him."

"Get this, that's who she pregnant from."

"Shet yo mouth and keep on talking. See there I knew that wasn't no Gavon baby. Ha! Thank you Jesus!!"

I was glad Gavon could finally get this girl out of his system. She was bad for anybody, now she had no reason to pop back up at my house. And boy if she did, had Gavon out here fighting because she wanted to be fast.

"Mama Jean I already called and got the bond for Gavon, don't worry about it I have it. They only charged him with disturbing the peace because I told them that Mario and Chardonnay came over to my house."

"Well praise God. I tell you the truth, I'm gone have to put Gavon on a curfew especially in my car. Here I was thinking he was home and he over there with you. Come on chile let's go get this nappy headed boy."

The ride to go and pick my car up was quiet, I wasn't gone bother him tonight but he owed me big time. I had to go see Alvin in the morning so I needed to rest up because I felt like something was off with him. Even when we had our talk on the phone a few nights ago he wasn't very talkative, he just wanted to make sure we got the letter.

Gavon was up and raking the yard when I left to go and see his father. I just gave him that look so he would know he better be home when I got back. I don't care how grown he was, as long as he stayed with me he was gone follow my rules.

I could believe even as an old woman I had to go through all this protocol stuff just to see my son in law. I missed my only daughter, I prayed for her and just like God gave her too me He took her. God was giving her warning after warning that her time was winding up. I thought Gavon was gone be her change but it only slowed her down but didn't stop her.

"Hey ma," Alvin squeezed me.

"You know I don't play about you looking like that. What's going on with you?"

"Ma I'm tired that's all. Why am I here, it's been twenty years mama. I miss my wife, I miss my son. I can't keep doing this. Did Gavon get my letter?"

The look in Alvin's eye's let me know he was at the end of his rope. I couldn't let him give up just like that. God was on the verge of changing his sons heart and I needed him here to see it.

"You talking nonsense now. Do you really think Danielle would want you to give up? Me and you both know Danielle would knock you upside your head if she heard you talking like this. As Danielle's mother I will not let you give up. You don't know this but Gavon got the letters from me last night. If you just give him some time to read them, I believe he will come around. Alvin don't give up, Gavon and I need you."

I smiled and I knew I brightened his mood. He had the most gorgeous smile, that's all Danielle would talk about. She would fuss with him and all he did was smile and her heart would soften up. Alvin was what Danielle needed, being raised in the streets with her brothers she needed someone that could handle her.

"You always had the perfect words to say when we are down. What we gone do when you leave this realm?"

"That's why I'm pouring everything into you. Gavon gone need you once I'm gone."

"Alright enough of that talk, you ain't going nowhere no time soon.

"Well your son went to jail last night for fighting."

"Say what now?" Alvin asked me.

"He's home. He has this cute little girl from the church that he has fallen for, but his ratchet little girlfriend was being messy cause he don't want her no more. As you can tell I don't like her," we both laughed. "She lied and said she was pregnant from Gavon, come to find out the dude she pregnant from likes the same girl Gavon likes. By the way her name is Chasiti."

"That boy got some drama going on. I hope this Chasiti girl can get him closer to God, them streets don't love him."

"I tried to tell him that."

Before my visit was over, I prayed for Alvin and ended up praying for at least four other inmates and their families. I don't know what God was doing behind the walls of the prison but from what everyone was telling me, Alvin was a big influence in the prison and that made me proud. I got back in my car and headed home to see where my grandson head was at.

Chasiti

"Papa I promise it was not Gavon's fault." I was trying to explain to papa what happen and he was livid when he came over to the house and I was still cleaning glass up and throwing out my end table that was broke from Gavon slamming Mario into it.

"I've told you to leave these hood boys alone. You not gone learn until it's too late. And I'm gone have a talk with Mama Jean about Gavon. I like Gavon but if he's gone be around I'm gone hold him accountable as a man. Now that Mario dude can no longer come around and if I see him

I'm gone shoot him in the foot about you now. Because from the sound of it, he brought drama to your house and I don't like that."

I knew Papa would go off, that's why I was trying to clean up everything before he popped up. Rev didn't play when it came to me and for a church leader he stayed strap. Because of so many recent church shootings he felt everyone's safety was the most important. So I knew he really would shoot Mario if it came down to it. I was done with him though, I knew he was a snake I was trying to figure it out and God brought it right to my front door. It's funny how that worked and I was relieved that Gavon wasn't the father of Chardonnay's baby. Now she was the one that I didn't want to pop back up because it was gone be on and popping. My papa helped me finish up the cleaning before he headed home.

I pulled my baked pork chops out of the oven and turned my green beans off on the stove. I was tired of cooking all this food and it was only me. I shot Gavon a text and asked him to come and eat with me. I didn't know if Mama Jean was gone let him hold the car so I called her and vouched for Gavon and I promised he wouldn't get in any trouble while with me. Mama Jean tripped me out, she even threatened me before we got off the phone. I loved that woman dearly. I knew Gavon would be here at any moment so I went ahead and fixed his plate and a cup of apple Kool-Aid.

"Hey," he kissed me when I opened the door for him. He had his dreads all over the place, I wasn't feeling that so I knew I was gone end up doing something to it by the end of the night.

"Dang you fixing a thug plate. I like this," he smiled at me. "Why you ain't got no man?"

"Oh trust boo boo I've had plenty of men, but the same men wanted me to put them first and I'm sorry, for me, God is first. They couldn't handle that so they left right before we were to get married. I came home and he was gone. So I said the next dude was gone be a man of God first before I even thought about getting in a relationship."

"I feel you ma. This is good, I didn't know you can throw down in the kitchen too. I was one of the guys that said I would never eat anyone food but Mama Jeans. We both know Mama Jean can burn."

"Yea you right," we laughed. "I'm assuming Chardonnay use to do your hair?"

"Please don't mention that girl name. But yea she used to twist it for me."

"Well let me get the kitchen clean and I'll get you right," I winked at him.

"Man that's what's up because Mama Jean threatened to cut them off while I was sleep if I didn't get them done."

We cleaned the kitchen together and I went and got my sit under dryer and clips. I washed Gavon dirty hair, it smelled just like marijuana. I needed to talk to him about his weed addiction too, he needed to let that mess go. I gave him a towels to wrap his hair up in and place on his shoulders while he sat between my legs. I started retwisting his dreads one by one. I clipped them and put him under the dryer he complained the whole time about it being too hot. I gave him a big fishtail braid down the middle of his back. Now he was looking like the Gavon I know.

"Thank you for doing that for me, I really appreciate it."

Gavon

I looked in the mirror downstairs and checked myself out. Chasiti had me looking right, I rubbed my chin and looked at it from different angles. I wondered where she learned how to do hair like that, her hair was always laid unless she had it in a ponytail.

"Boy you ain't cute," Mama Jean pushed me in my back.

"Mama you know I look good," I gave her my famous smile.

"Yea you do look good son. Just like your daddy, and boy when you smile I think I'm looking right at Alvin." Mama Jean laid her head on my chest, I loved when she did that. I wrapped my arms around her and she returned the favor. Mama Jean was my world, after she had that little talk with me.

"You welcome. I have your letters here too I don't want you to leave them because I really want you read them." I gave them to him and gave him a hug goodnight.

I locked up for the night and retreated to get in the shower, I was sore from twisting all his thick hair. I let the hot beads of water hit my body as I lathered my soap on my wash cloth. I had two more days of suspension left before I could go back to work. I truly missed work because it gave me the opportunity to be around different people. This was the most time I ever spent in the house. I was thinking about going to sit with Mama Jean tomorrow and see if she had anything for me to do around the house. I got in my bed and had a conversation with God about my future.

I hadn't even hung out in the hood, I stayed home with her. Her mentioning my father made me touch my back pocket where all my letters were. She had them wrapped in a rubber because it was so many of them.

"I love you Gavon you know that don't you?" She looked up at me.

"I know Mama Jean and I love you too."

"That's what I like to hear," she released me.

I walked up to my room and closed the door. I pulled the wad of letters out and opened the second letter. This letter was dated when I was five, I wasn't sure why there was a gap but I opened it and his picture fell out. I looked at it examining every detail about my father, he had the dreads and the same smile. No wonder Mama Jean said what she said. It was like looking at myself. I put the picture on my dresser and opened the letter.

Dear Gavon:

I can't believe you are five already. I called you on your birthday but Mama Jean said you were wore out from your birthday party. I told Mama Jean to send me some pictures of you so if grandma ask you to take a picture don't act silly. Make sure you listen to Mama Jean and don't talk back, just do as she says. She told me you are doing good your first year in school, I'm proud to be your father. I love you and don't ever forget it son. I hope to see you soon.

Love Daddy

I couldn't stand to read another letter tonight. I knew this was gone be something that was gone take some time. One thing I knew for sure is that my daddy loved me. I don't know why I was getting soft. I took a quick shower and went downstairs to check on my grandma. She was sitting in her chair reading her Bible.

"Come on down son," she looked up.

"Nah I don't want to bother you."

"You not bothering me, now get down here."

I walked down the stairs and sat in the other chair. As she finished up her scripture, I instantly hated that I didn't bring my phone down her to scroll Facebook.

"I see you reading your letters," she said without looking up from the Bible.

"How you know," I looked at her crazy.

"Because earlier when I said you look like you father, you didn't give me any lip."

Mama Jean read me good, I couldn't even say anything.

"Well I'm about to head to bed and rub this ole knee with some bengay," Mama Jean said and I laughed. "You laughing now but you gone get old you know that right?"

"Ma I know. Come on let me help you," I helped her raise up from her chair. Once I heard her close her room door I locked the front and back door and went to bed.

———

The smell of bacon woke me slap up out my sleep. I wiped the slob from my mouth and stretched. I went into my bathroom and handle myself before heading downstairs. *Who Mama Jean talking too?* I walked into the kitchen to see Chasiti in the kitchen cooking breakfast while Mama Jean sat at the table running her mouth.

"Well good morning Gavon," Mama Jean said looking at me nodding her head towards Chasiti. I shook my head at my grandma, she was a trip.

"I'm just about done if you want to sit down Gee," Chasiti said. I sat next to Mama Jean and she winked at me.

"So Chasiti what you got planned today?" Mama Jean asked her.

"I was gone hang with you today, see if you had anything for me to do."

"Oh I got plenty for you to do baby. I need to send you and Gavon to the store, I got some greens that need to be picked and cut for Sunday too."

"Ok whatever you need me to do."

Oh Mama Jean was laying it on thick. She was making it her business to have us spend as much time as possible together. I was cool with it though. After breakfast Mama Jean gave us this long list of stuff to go and get from the store. We took Chasiti car and went to the store after getting back Mama Jean was on the porch with her peas and greens. I put the groceries up while Chasiti stopped on the porch to start picking the greens.

Chardonnay

I was sitting back watching Gavon and Chasiti at the grocery store like they were a couple. I was pissed at little Ms. Piggy it was because of her that Mario shut me completely off, he changed his number and everything. And now Gavon was looking happy and even had his hair done. I wonder did thickums do it. I was feeling brave so I was gone go home and change and head down to Mama Jean house. I had some stuff to get off my chest, now that I was no longer with Gee, Mama Jean was gone be the first one that was gone get a whiff of these pregnancy hormones and then I was just gone go down the line. Whoever wanted it could get it, it was whatever to me at this point. I had nothing else to lose. I hated to go over there and show them real crazy but I think Chasiti thought I was somebody to play with. Gee knows how I get down so if he knew better when I get there he better tell his fat pig to stay in her place.

I went home and changed into some sweats and tennis shoes and pulled my real hair in a ponytail. I was tense because I couldn't continue to get my hair and stuff done so I was wearing my real hair and I didn't have any edges, I slicked them back as best as I could. I grabbed my Vaseline and put some on my face. I didn't know if Chasiti was gone swing or not but I didn't want any scratches. This was my fourth pregnancy and I've fought every time so this wasn't gone be any different. I snatched my keys up and headed a few blocks up the road to this old hag's house.

Gavon

After leaving the store with Chasiti and getting everything unloaded I got a text from my uncle Reno asking me to come by. He said that he and my other uncle wanted to talk to me. It's been a while since I last kicked it with my family and it would do me some good to spend time with them. I just hated that we couldn't do it like Mama Jean wanted us to. Although they were deep in the streets from what I was told, after my mom passed they went even harder.

The two of them ran the streets of Savannah with an iron fist but they were also discrete with it. My mom was older than them so she was the one who taught her little brothers the game. It sounded backwards to me because normally you would have the man running things but this was the other way around. It worked like a charm though all the way up until she took her last breath.

I grabbed Mama Jean's car keys and headed out to the porch.

"Where you going baby?" she asked me looking up as she snapped the peas in her bowl in half. Chasiti was sitting beside her on the floor peeling the greens and throwing the stems into a Wal-Mart bag. I just admired them and how well they got along and I knew that the decision I made to move on from Chardonnay was the best one I could have ever made. She would never be accepted into our family like Chasiti was. Not because Mama Jean wouldn't allow it but because Chardonnay wouldn't allow herself to try.

"Uncle Reno text me and asked me to come by so I'm gonna run through real quick." I told her. I could see her eyes begin to get moist when I mentioned her oldest son's name. She missed them so much and it hurt her that she couldn't see them on the regular. But there was one thing that she didn't compromise anything for and that was God.

No matter how much she loved a person, if it took away from putting Him first she would cut you off with the quickness.

"Baby be careful please. And let your uncles know that I love them." she said.

"I will mama. Chas you good?" I said turning my attention to her as she smiled.

"Yeah boo I'm ok. Just be careful like Mama said and come back home to us."

This is the type of stuff that makes a man fall in love. I couldn't put my finger on it but Chasiti had my head gone. I kissed her on her forehead before getting in the car and backing out of the driveway. I blew the horn before bending the block. As I drove towards the other side of town I began to think about the letters that my old man had sent me. I was torn about what could possibly be in them and if I even wanted to hear an explanation from him. So many years had gone by and I just wasn't sure anymore.

I pulled up to the neighborhood my uncles lived in and Yamacraw Village was jumping. I saw both of my uncles chopping it up with their crew as I was parking the car. I knew no one would bother Mama Jean's car. Not because of my uncles but because they respected her so much. Any given day she could come over this way and no one would bother her unless they wanted a hug or words of encouragement. They loved her like their own. I knew even though my uncles wouldn't change their lives the way she wanted them to, they loved her unconditionally.

"What it do nephew?" my uncle Danny said giving me dap and embracing me followed by my uncle Reno.

"Can't call it." I said back to them and acknowledging their friends as well.

Uncle Reno said that they would get up with them later and the three of us walked inside his house. I could smell the chicken being fried so I knew his girl Rasheeda was in there putting it down. I sat down on the couch and looked around the nicely decorated living room. Unk wasn't doing too bad for himself. I just didn't know why he decided to stay here after all of these years. Something about not wanting to be a sell out just because he had some money. I didn't understand that method of thinking because the first chance I got to get up on some money I was moving my grandmother away from the hood and into a real nice neighborhood. She deserved it because she put her life on hold for me and I couldn't wait to pay her back.

I looked at all of the pictures of our family on his wall and smiled at the one of my mother holding me as a baby with my father kissing her on her cheek while they both smiled at me. I wished that things had turned out differently but here we were over twenty years later and it still felt fresh.

"So what's going on youngin'?" Danny asked me. He was the enforcer of the family. He stood 6'4 and weighed almost 300 pounds. He kept his hair in neat locks like mine and they hung almost to his butt. The ladies loved them so he always made sure to keep them done. He had dark brown eyes and we shared the same milk chocolate complexion but he was a part of the beard gang as we called it. His beard was so long it could be braided up if he chose to. Reno looked like the both of us in the face only he had a low cut with waves and a neat go-tee. Danny and Reno were the same height except Reno weighed a little less. Around 225 or so.

"Man I'm just chilling trying to get to this money." I laughed reaching for the blunt Danny offered me. I took a long drag and almost bust my chest open.

"Runt you better slow down. That's that fire right there." he said calling me by my nickname. I was a preemie when I was born and that was his name for me because I was so small.

I got myself together and was able to finally catch my breath. I sat back on the couch and wiped the tears that fell from my eyes as Rasheeda brought me a cup of water.

"Don't be in here letting your uncles kill you with this death weed. Then I'm gonna have to explain to Mama what happened." she said laughing. My aunt was really pretty. Her hair was long and natural and she kept it twisted high on her head. She was light skinned and had eyes that were so dark they looked black. Whenever I came around she always treated me like her own and I loved her for that.

"Ain't nobody trying to kill him. He wanted to hang with the big boys so he gotta do big boy things." Reno laughed. Rasheeda gave him the side eye and left us alone to go and check on her food.

"So what's good unk? What was so important that I needed to come over here?" I asked. Seeing my aunt in the kitchen cooking and how she took care of home made me think about Chasiti and I was ready to get back to her. If it had been any other time I would have kicked back for a while since it had been a minute that I got to hang with them. Ever since the stabbing I had been MIA for a while.

"Well we called you over here because we wanted to see what was going on? I heard you had been stabbed but by the time we found out and we came to visit you they said you were already discharged." he informed me.

"And you know how mama feels about us and our lifestyle so we couldn't come over there. So we figured that it would be best to give you time to heal then we would reach out." Danny added.

"Yeah I got caught slipping that one time." I said thinking back on what happened and getting mad all over again.

"One time? Word on the street is that you keep slipping."

"What you talking about?" I said getting upset. The streets sure knew how to talk.

"What happened with that Po Cat situation?" Danny asked me.

"Man unc I hit this lick with him for 50 g's and this bum only gave me 5 stacks." I fumed as I sat back still angry.

"See what I mean? You slipping. Had you been on your grown man hustle ain't no way he would have been able to get over on you. Then you let that broad Chardonnay set you up for the nigga yall robbed," he said shocking me. I should have known that they would find out what happened but I didn't think they would go that deep and know so much. I had been slipping when I sat there and thought about it.

"Nephew look. I'm gonna be honest with you. This life ain't for you," Reno said getting straight to the point.

"What you mean? I'm bout this life," I said angrily. I felt like they were calling me soft and I didn't like it. Everybody underestimated me but if the truth be told some days I underestimated myself.

"Calm down Runt, we not saying this to make you mad or make you feel like less of a man. All we are saying is that this street life isn't for you. Danielle is probably turning over in her grave because we didn't stop you sooner. After Alvin went down for her murder we should have stepped in and helped mama raise you to be what your parents wanted. We dropped the ball but not anymore. You could have been dead and I feel like it would have been our fault. Mama only could do so much and

Alvin tried but you gave him a hard time." Danny

jumped in.

The thought of them being so calm when

they talked about my father shocked me. We never

had a conversation about how they felt about him

and what he did. I thought they should be angry like

I was but it seemed like out of everyone around me

I was the only one holding him accountable.

"Why is it that I'm the only one mad at him

for what he did?" I was tired of everyone being on

his side.

"Because none of us believe he did it but

you. Alvin loved your mother Gavon and tried his

best to get her out of these streets but she was

stubborn."

"Just like someone else I know," Rasheeda

said coming out of the kitchen with plates in her

hand. It smelled good but I had lost my appetite, I had too much on my mind.

"So if he didn't do it then who did and why aren't they sitting behind bars instead of him?" I asked.

"Because they only went on what it looked like, you know how these pigs are. As long as they cuffed someone they didn't care who it was."

"So yall really don't think he was responsible?" This was too much information and I was at a loss for words. If what my uncles were saying was true then that meant my mother's murderer was still out there.

"Not at all, but we also don't know what went on in the house that night for sure."

"Listen nephew get out while you still can."

"That's easy for yall to say, yall pockets are fat and mine are hurting. I know I can come to yall for help but I'm a grown man and I got to do this on my own," I said standing up to leave. I needed to clear my head.

"Runt listen to me," Danny said as Reno got up and went to the back. "I feel you on wanting to be a man and take care of yourself but we family and we are here for you. This is not your calling in life and it's not in you to be a street cat. There is something more out there for you and we just want you to make it. I'm sorry we were so wrapped up in this business and haven't been there like you needed us to be, but it's time for us to be there now. Mama may not have been able to stop us from getting into the dope gang but you are what she's fighting so hard for. She knows there is greater in you than you can see right now. Everybody sees it but you."

Reno came back into the living room with an envelope in his hand and stood before me.

"In this life we must always be prepared no matter what and at any given moment you could be taken away living how we do. You know tomorrow isn't guaranteed especially for a street cat," he said handing me the envelope.

"Your mother was well prepared for anything and she wanted to make sure that if something happened to her that you and Alvin would be straight. Danielle hated how she couldn't let the streets go like he wanted her to. That man worked so hard because he felt like if he could keep providing her with the life she was accustomed to then she would leave it alone. Right before her murder she had set up an interest baring bank account in your name. Your mother was smart and knew that having a safe or duffle bags full of money in a floorboard of her house wouldn't do you any good. That's why I think that she was killed. Someone probably thought she kept money there and when they couldn't get what they came for she had to reap what she had sown."

"Take this money and do something positive with it. Go back to college and pick up a trade or something. Help mama like you always talked about. Maybe even buy you a house and marry your little girlfriend." Rasheeda said reappearing again, she was just like a jack-in-the-box, popping up when you least expected it.

"I'm not with Chardonnay anymore Auntie." I told her.

"Oh I'm not talking about that little heffa, I meant Chasiti," she said with a huge smile on her face. I looked at both of my uncles and they both wore the same silly expressions.

"How yall know about Chasiti?" I asked. She didn't run the streets or sleep around so I wondered who was snitching. This just further proved their point that I was slipping. Had I really been on my A game I would know who was watching me or her.

"Cause my cousin Donna works at the hospital where she works. She was there the night you came in but it took her a minute to remember who you were. But when she did a few days later she called me right away. Since then she says that all Chasiti talks about is you." Rasheeda stated.

The smile was so big on my face just thinking about her that my cheeks hurt. To know that she was feeling me like I was feeling her did something to my heart and I was nervous yet happy about it.

"Nephew she's good for yo, let her in and give her all of you. Be the man of God that you were called to be for her. And I better get an invite to the wedding and baby showers." she laughed kissing my cheek and walking out again.

My uncles and I just laughed at her before I gave them dap and headed to the door. Before I could make it completely out, Reno stopped me.

"Nephew."

"What up unc?"

"Don't worry about the get back. Po Cat and Mario will be taken care of. You feel me?" he said making sure I understood where he was coming from. After all that they had just dropped on me all I could do was nod my head. I didn't know if I could fully let the streets go but I would do my best to try not just for my family but for my girl. I was going to make Chasiti mine before it was all over with.

Chasiti

Spending time with Mama Jean was always so much fun and full of wisdom being shared from her to me. She told me about her life as a young girl, how she dealt with certain situations, and even when she was frustrated with God. The way she would always call on him in good times and bad you would think she never felt that way.

When Gavon came out of the house and said that he was going to see his uncles, I noticed the hurt look on her face. She missed her children so much that it hurt her to her very core but she knew that she couldn't be around them. It would take a miracle for them to start walking right. I just prayed that she would get to see it before her assignment here on earth was up.

Looking at Gavon gave me such a warm feeling inside whenever I was around him. I didn't know what it was but I was falling hard and I wasn't sure if I wanted to stop. When he looked at me he looked like I was the most beautiful girl in the world and treated me like that too. The more time we spent together the harder I prayed that this was what God had planned for us. So far He hasn't let me know otherwise but that didn't always mean that God was giving His approval. I believed sometimes He got quiet and let us handle the situation ourselves, then later reveal His plan to us. Either we were going to make the right decision or wrong one but the choice was ours.

People get mad at God when bad things happen and want to blame Him but in all actuality it's not His fault. He gives us free will and our decisions and actions that we make are going to either hurt or help us. It's when we think we know it all and mess up we don't want to take any accountability for what we did. So it's easier to blame someone else and most times we blame Him. Yet He still loves us and gives us more grace and mercy although we don't even deserve it. Who wouldn't want to serve a God like that?

I was taken away from my thoughts when he kissed me on my forehead before heading to the car and leaving.

"Mmmm I guess I need to start getting me a wedding outfit ready," Mama said.

"What are you talking about lady?" I asked her trying to play it off. I knew what she was referring to because the thought had definitely crossed my mind about one day marrying Gavon.

"Don't play with me chile, I know the look of love when I see it. And it's all over the both of you." she answered while snapping another bean in half.

"I don't know what you are referring to," I blushed. I was doing a horrible job of covering my feelings for him up.

"Baby you might as well put that leaf down, hold your arms out to the Lord, and repent for that bold face lie that just came out of your mouth." she snickered.

"How can you tell?" I wanted to know.

"Because that's the same way I used to look at my late husband, bless his soul. When you were about thirteen is when I started to see the look in both you and Gavon's eyes."

"What? I barely knew him then and we were so young."

"So what? When genuine love hits you age doesn't matter. What matters is if you are ready to handle it when it comes."

"What do you mean?" I asked her. She had my full attention now and I wanted to see what she schooled me on next.

"What I mean is you can be thirteen or a hundred and thirteen, but if you are not ready to take those feeling seriously not just for you but the other person as well it will never work. Why do you thinks so many marriages fail? It's because no one took the time to cultivate and allow God to lead them in the decisions they made before marriage.

No one courts anyone anymore like back in the day. See we took the time to get to know one another and to understand each other. You have to not just fall in love with someone you have to fall in like with them as well. People think that love is all you need but that is not so. You may love someone but you can't stand the person they are on the inside. And if you took the time before jumping in the sack with one another then that bond that you have now created clouds your judgement. Why do you think that God wanted us to wait until after marriage that you lay with someone? By then you have both had the time to not only cultivate your relationship with each other but the connection and relationship with God will be stronger.

Now don't get me wrong, just because you may fall short in that area and not wait until marriage doesn't mean that person is not for you. Trust I didn't wait until I was married to drop it like it was hot," she said doing a little bounce in her rocking chair that had me rolling.

"Temptation is out there but in the end it may just work out. But it can be so much easier if we would just take the time to know ourselves first and then the other person. I knew when I saw that look in your eyes as well as his that this would be God's will for the both of you. It was just at the time neither of you were ready."

"He was looking at me the same way?" I asked shocked.

"Girl you are cheesing just like a little chester cat." I laughed at her because I always heard people say "chester cat" instead of "cheshire cat".

"When Mitch and I saw those looks we knew it was only a matter of time before the two of you got together but we prayed it would be when the both of you were ready. I think that time has come."

"Wait Papa knows?" I panicked. He has never said anything about knowing my true feelings for Gavon.

"Yeaaa he knows chile. You know us old school goons for the Lord be knowing."

I almost passed out from that "goons for the Lord." This woman was a trip. I remember the time she was talking about like it had just happened yesterday. It was right before my fourteenth birthday and we were just wrapping up youth church one Sunday. I knew who Gavon was and although our grandparents were friends we never hung out. Whenever we went by Mama Jean's house he was never there. Always in the streets with his friends. But this particular day was different. It was just something about him that I couldn't put my finger on but he was different.

We both stayed behind to help clean up and get the church back in order. The more we talked the more I started to realize I liked him. From that day on I would pray that God would let him come to church each time the doors were opened, and with the exception of a few times over the years, he was there. Then one day it just stopped, I learned from Mama Jean that Chardonnay was in his life. That explained the disappearance. It wasn't like we were a couple so what could I say. I was disappointed but my way of getting over him was to move on and that's what I did. I just moved on to the wrong dude.

Mama Jean was still talking but I hadn't heard a word she said, my mind was so boggled with thoughts of the past that I had zoned out. I had zoned back in just in time to see Chardonnay come barreling down the street in her car and I knew this was about to be some mess. I could feel it.

Chardonnay got out of her car looking like she was ready for war and before either of us could speak she went off on Mama Jean first.

"Listen here you old bat!" she started.

"Ya mammy a bat."

"Mama Jean!" I said shocked at her comeback.

"What chile? She bout blind as one too. And talking bout uglyyyyyy! Ha! Chardonnay chile what happened to yo' edges? They real smooth and clean like a baby's bottom. I told you bout all them tracks with that black glue. Done messed around and snatched the last of the hair follicles you had."

"Ohhhh Mama Jean." I cried. She was going in and there was nothing that Chardonnay could say. This old lady had cracked her face picked it up for her and cracked it again. I was so weak in my body from laughing I was dizzy.

"Then she got the nerve to have it pulled tight in a lil ball. Looking like a Rottweiler tail." That did it and before I could react she was charging full speed ahead at mama.

Mama Jean

Chardonnay must have forgotten bout me. I ain't been old and had bad knees all my life so when needed I could go toe to toe with the best of them in a fist fight. She messed around and underestimated me by charging me but I caught her one good time square in her nose to back her up off of me and give me enough time to get to my feet. If I hadn't been paying attention she may have got me but like the old man in the State Farm commercial, she had to be quicker than that.

Just as she was coming back at me and before I got all the way up Chasiti jumped in.

"Oh no you don't!" she yelled as she served a mean two piece right to Chardonnay's face. The two of them were going at it so hard but my girl had the upper hand. I saw people coming out on their porches to see the fight and that's when I realized I had to stop it. I didn't want Chasiti to get into any trouble and I knew it was just a matter of time before someone called the police. I wasn't worried because Chardonnay was on my property and Chasiti was a guest in my home. If anyone was going to jail it wasn't Chas and I was going to make sure of that.

"Junior come help me get my baby off of her." I yelled to my next door neighbor's grandson. He was around Alvin's age and I was glad that he was visiting his father that day.

It took him a few minutes to get them apart just as the sirens got louder. I knew someone would call them it was only a matter of time. Chardonnay must have had something on her because once she figured out the law was on their way she got in that clunker she had and dipped out just as fast as she had come. I was going to tell the police to not worry about filing a police report because I knew she wouldn't be coming back.

I eased back up on the porch and just as I was about to sit down I felt like an elephant had just sat on my chest. My arm started tingling and the pain intensified as I lifted my arm to signal I was in need. The pain was so bad all I could do was groan in agony. I heard cars screeching to a halt and Chasiti running to me right before I hit the ground. All I could do was pray that God welcomed me home.

Gavon

I was laying in my bed looking up at the ceiling. I had yet to take my suit off and I didn't want to be bothered. I had just laid to rest the woman that gave her all for her family. What was I going to do now that she was no longer here? I heard my uncles downstairs talking to our guests. Mama Jean impacted so many people's lives through the years so of course her funeral was packed with them wanting to give their final goodbyes.

When I got back to the house that day after leaving my uncle's house I drove around just trying to get my head wrapped around everything they had filled me in on. Had I just went straight home maybe I could have stopped the attack on her by Chardonnay. I knew she had heard what happened and it was her fault that my grandmother was cold and laying in the dirt. I went by her house that night after signing for her body to be taken to the funeral home and she was nowhere to be found. The next day I went by all of her things were gone and I knew she was in hiding. If she knew like I knew then she better hide forever cause when I caught her I was going to be catching a charge for murdering her.

My door opened and I didn't even need to move to know who it was. The fragrance of Vera Wang's Princess hit my nose and calmed me even before her soothing voice did.

"Hey baby." Chasiti said coming to sit on the bed beside me. I didn't even respond with words, I just motioned for her to lay with me. Chasiti kicked off her shoes as she climbed beside me. This was the first time she had been in my room. Mama Jean didn't play that having women upstairs in her house if we weren't married. I chuckled at the thought of her.

"I'm glad you're able to smile, I miss your smile but I understand," she said looking up at me.

She had been taking this hard just like me and I knew it was because of the bond she had with my grandma. They were so close and loved each other just the same. I looked down into her puffy red eyes and wiped the tears that were still falling. I wanted to stop her pain but I didn't even know how to stop my own.

"I was just thinking about how grandma always blocked me from having women over in my room and now here you are." I explained.

"She definitely did not play about that. Mama loved me but she told me I wasn't coming up here until we were married. That would only be to help you move your stuff out." she laughed. I loved the sound of that and it was soothing to my soul.

"I guess she's mad at us now huh?"

"I doubt it. She knows that you need me and I want to be here for you."

"What am I going to do without her?" I wasn't really asking her for an answer and I think she realized that so she didn't respond.

We stayed in that position for a few minutes longer just listening to one another breathe and the sounds of our heartbeats beating to the same rhythm before she said anything.

"Baby?"

"Hmm?" I responded waiting on her to talk. With all of my family downstairs she was the only one that I wanted to talk to right now.

"Don't wait until it's too late like your uncles did."

I was confused and I guess my silence reflected that. Chasiti sat up and motioned for me to do the same. She scooted up to my headboard and motioned for me to lay my head in her lap. Twisting my hair she began to explain what she meant.

"All of these years that went by and your uncles are now hurting so bad that they didn't' make it right with their mother. Although she never held any hatred in her heart for them they know they should have been here for her. Now she's gone and it's eating them up. It's going to take some time for them to get over this and I don't want that happening to you." she explained.

I knew Uncle Danny and Reno loved their mother but they were so caught up in the street life that they just felt like she was trying to change them instead of taking time to understand where she was coming from. Because they didn't have a relationship with God they couldn't grasp what she was telling them.

"But what does that have to do with me? I was here for her."

"Yes baby, you were, she was so glad to have you here. She felt like you were the last one that she could save. Mama told me on more than one occasion that you were her last assignment and it would be you that would carry this family. It's time for you to make amends with your father. I just pray that it isn't too late." she said.

"Too late for what Chas?" I was confused as to what she was talking about. Instead of responding to me she pulled out an envelope from her pants pocket and handed it to me. I looked and saw that it was a letter from my father that was recent. She had made it over to the door I guess to

give me some privacy but I didn't want to be alone.
I knew I had been slacking on reading all of his
letters but there was so many and I was scared that
one of them would contain something about my
mother I didn't want to know.

"Stay with me?" I asked looking up to her.

She smiled and said, "Of course."

I ripped open the letter, took a deep breath,
and began reading out loud.

To my son,

*I have this feeling that by
now you still haven't read all of my other letters.
Mama told me that you read a couple of the ones
that I wrote when you were a child but not any of
the ones that I really wanted you to read. I
understand that you felt like I hurt your mother but*

Gavon please believe me when I say that I loved you and your mother more than life itself. All I wanted was for her to get out of the game and I would take care of any and everything that she needed me to do. She just couldn't let go.

And now I feel it's time for me to let go. I've been in here for over twenty years hoping and praying to either to be exonerated because of my innocence or to have you come and see me. I've spent the last of my savings that I had to get a new legal team to open my case again. I go once more before the board next month and I've come to terms that if I'm not proven to be innocent then my time here on earth is done. I know that Mama always prays for me and says to give her a little more time to talk to you but I don't want to force anything on you. I understand that you are hurt and confused and I'm not upset at all at you. I just want to let you know that I always have and always will love you and you can rest in knowing that. Don't feel like this is your fault that I rather put myself out of this misery, but it's too painful to bare any longer.

Gavon I love you with every fiber of my being and I want you to make sure that pretty young lady Mama told me about is taken care of. I heard she really loves you and I know she is good for you. Make me a grandfather and tell my grandkids that their Gramps loved them even before they entered the world. And my daughter in law Chasiti too. I'm proud of you son. You didn't end up in here or dead and that was my biggest concern.

Oh and please make sure that your old man is sharp when they lay me to rest.

Love Dad

By the time I finished reading I was sick to my stomach and couldn't stop the tears from falling. Chasiti held me tight just letting me get it all out. It was then that I understood that if anything happened to my father and I didn't make it right with him I would be going through exactly what my uncles were now and I couldn't take it. I just prayed I wasn't too late. I heard paper rustling and looked up just as Chasiti began to speak.

"Babe look. He put the date, time, and which courtroom he would be in. He goes tomorrow morning at nine. I believe God is extending time for the two of you." she said as I felt the weight of the world lift.

"That's my baby. See I told you that God would get the glory." I heard Mama Jean say. I looked towards where her voice came from and there she was standing in all white. She didn't have a cane and she was glowing.

"Remember baby I will always be with you in spirit. I love you," she said before she vanished. I had a feeling that she would pop up every so often to keep me in check but as long as she did that I would never feel alone.

"All rise!" I heard as Chasiti, my uncles, Reverend Rockmore and I stood outside of courtroom number three. I was so nervous because once I opened those doors my life would change. Maybe for the good and maybe it would be all bad either way I wasn't going to find out standing in the hallway. I took a deep breath and opened the door quietly. We all filed in and went unnoticed as we sat on the two back rows. I couldn't get any closer because my feet felt like they were weighed down so this row was as far as I could get. I noticed my uncles looking over to the other side of the room and I followed their eyes. There was Mario and another gentleman that were sitting in the corner.

They kept whispering to each other and looking over at my father with smirks on their faces and that piqued my interest. The judge was still talking about what would be happening today but all I could do was focus on Mario and the man. The man sitting beside him kept rubbing the scar that he had on the back of his neck that looked like a burn mark. They sat a few more minutes before slipping out of the side door. When they slipped out so did my uncles. I knew something was up but I wasn't capable of getting up right then to go and find out what it was. Chasiti held my hand and gave me a smile as the judge had my father stand up.

"Your honor my client has depleted all of his funds to have his case reopened. But I do believe that my client is innocent." his public defender stated. The look on my father's face told a story of years of pain and sleepless nights and one look at him and I knew that he wasn't responsible for my mother being murdered. I don't know what it was but it was like God was telling me that he was just as much a victim as my mother and I were.

"We don't have the time to waste tax payers money trying to open up a case for someone who is guilty." said the prosecutor. I could tell she was out for blood by her demeanor. She didn't play and nine times out of ten she won her cases. I had so many homeboys get locked up behind her it wasn't funny.

If my father had a chance to get out he would need the best of the best to get him out.

"I'll pay." I said shocking everyone in the courtroom including myself. All eyes were on me but the ones that I locked with belonged to my father. The look on his face as he closed his eyes and broke down in tears created a water fall to flow from mine.

"And you are?" the prosecutor asked.

"This is Mr. Cunningham's son. Your honor can we receive a recess?" his defender asked.

"We will reconvene at one o'clock." the judge said as he hit the gavel on his stand.

I felt the cement on my feet being removed as I walked towards my father's table in the front. He still had his eyes closed and he was crying and speaking in tongues. I touched him gently on his shoulder not knowing what else to do and he reached up and placed his on top of mine. I felt his hand trembling as he squeezed mine. He stood up and we just stared at each other for a few seconds before I welcomed his embrace as we cried like two babies.

It was time for me to sit down and hear my father out. He was innocent and I knew this wasn't where he belonged. I looked up and saw the biggest smile on my grandmother's face as she vanished. With that God let me know he was coming home.

Alvin

After so many years of praying to God about my son, He finally showed me that He works things out in his own time. I'd just got over being sick about Mama Jean's death, I felt like I lost my mother. She was there for so many of us, when Danielle and I first got married we had to live with her until I got on my feet. Mama Jean never for once made me feel less of a man because I couldn't find work. As I held on to my son, all his pain from over the years was oozing out of his body. I didn't want to let him go until it was all out.

"Come on son, let's sit. You know I don't have much time and I want to get to know you better before I get thrown back in the cage," I told him. We sat and for the first time I was able to see the real resemblance. Gavon was me all over again. A smiled crossed my face because the whole time Danielle was pregnant she didn't want to be bothered with me unless she was hungry.

"Dad I'm…I don't know what to say," Gavon finally spoke.

"Son just let me say, thank you. All I ever wanted was to see you. I could spend the rest of my life in here but all I wanted was you. God has been good to me, even in here. I haven't got into any trouble, and He has sent people in my path to make sure I was well taken care of."

"I see Mama Jean got you too huh," he laughed.

"Got me what?"

"Saved."

"You better believe it. That woman will pray you through anything."

"Yea she would do that," Gavon held his head down.

"Son she wouldn't want you sad like this here. You hold your head up. Your grandmother did an excellent job in raising you."

"I miss her that's all, I feel bad because I left her at home that day. I should've been there!"

"You're going to always miss her son. Don't blame yourself, God needed that woman with Him more than you needed her. You're still young and the older you get, you'll understand the will of God. Enough of the sadness, I see you and your pretty lady kicking pretty hard huh?" I smiled at him.

"Yea, she's slowly helping me to change, I can't even describe the feeling."

"That's love son," I stated. I hated I wasn't there to have that talk with him, but I'm pretty sure Mama Jean handled that for me.

"So I haven't read any of the other letters but I'm curious to know what happen that night. I have nightmares of what I seen," Gavon looked at me.

I let out a sigh. It was always hard for me to relive that night. I had prepared myself for this talk, the last time I seen my son physically was me yelling for him to go back in his room. Today I realized that I never verbally talked about it, I had only wrote it down on paper for Gavon. I let all those years past and never went to counseling or anything. It was time to get it out verbally, I owed my son that much as he sat there looking at me.

"All I can tell you is what I walked in on. I came home from work late, your mama **saw** this nice dress she wanted for our anniversary. I wanted to buy it before she went out and got it. She was always hard headed," I chuckled.

"I bet."

"When I walked in that night I saw a male standing over your mama's battered body. Before I could pull my gun from my back he shot her in the head, I was able to get one shot off before he ran out the back door. I know I hit that cat because before they cuffed me there were droplets of blood that didn't belong to your mama." I clenched the side of my jaw. I was saved now but I knew if I ever found out who it was, I wanted to kill them with my bare hands. Twenty years of sitting here still hadn't took that bitterness away.

"Mr. Cunningham it's time to get back in the courtroom." I stood up to be cuffed and looked at Gavon one last time. He stood and nodded his head at me. I didn't know where he got the money from but if he was willing to help me become a free man, I was gone let him do what he had to do.

"Mr. Cunningham, we decided to open the case back up. From the look of the evidence there was no collection of blood, the gun you had was taken for evidence but was not brought up in the evidence, and I see where they took DNA from your wife but the results were not mentioned in the trial. We will adjourn back here in one week to set a date for the trial," he hit the gavel. I looked at my son and his crew with tears in my eyes as I was escorted back to my cage. When I made back to my cell I fell to my knees and looked up thanking God. He was answering my prayers, who would've knew Mama Jean leaving the earth would bring everyone together like it did. My talk with my son went better than I thought it would. *Thank you Mama Jean.* I could heather telling me, *God is gonna do it.*

Chardonnay

I pulled the curtains back to my motel room.
I wasn't expecting things to go left on me. Gavon
was after me, Mario was sending threats about
fighting and pregnant with his baby. I opened the
door for the pizza guy. I gave him the $10.13,
snatched my pizza and slammed and locked the
door back. I had five dollars left to last me I didn't
know what I was going to do but I knew I couldn't
just sit in this room and figure it out. I was in
Pooler, Ga. so I didn't expect anyone to notice me. I
missed my doctor's appointment and Mario had just
sent a text asking where I was. I hadn't broken the
news to Mario that I wasn't pregnant, I was playing
him too. I ordered a pregnant suit offline. I needed
to go back and get some of my bags and jewelry to
pawn but I didn't want to chance being seen. I
turned the square television on and started eating

my pizza. My phone buzzed, I placed my slice of pizza in the box and wiped my hands on the side of my pants and picked my phone up.

Gee: I know where you hiding. Yo best bet is to get back to Savannah for you and your baby be floating in Tybee Island.

I started laughing. Gee knew he wasn't about that life, he didn't even know how to hold a gun. I was about to be real petty and play this game with him.

Me: Who said I wasn't in Savannah? You can't be looking for me too hard. Find you a highway and go play in traffic punk.

Gee: Okay so that wasn't you that just grabbed the pizza. You in Pooler right? Travelodge Suites? I suggest you don't play with

me. **Never underestimate me. I'll see you in Savannah tomorrow.**

I slightly pulled my curtain back and I saw an all-black crown vic with the tint so dark you couldn't see through it. Only thing I could see was him pulling on his blunt. I slowly closed the curtain and made sure the lock was on the door. *How did he find out where I was?* I decided to text Mario to pick me up.

Me: Hey could you come get me? My car won't start.

Mario: Nah you on your own. You not my girl.

I closed the pizza box and sat it on the desk. I started plotting my escape. I was gone wait until he left so I could go somewhere else. Something told me to go to Rincon, he would've never found me there. I started throwing everything in my bag. I took a shower and put on something comfortable. I needed to go home and get some of my bags to sell to get another room in Rincon and get some gas. It was now 2:12am and the coast was clear. I slipped out and left the motel key on the dresser. I got behind my wheel and drove back to Savannah to grab a few things. When I made it back I drove pass Mama Jean house to see if her car was in the yard. Her car was there but that wasn't the car I seen at the hotel. I didn't want to draw to much attention so I drove down the block to my apartment.

I parked down at another building and walked down to my apartment. I had my taser in one hand and my house key in the other hand. I was mad because I forgot to leave my porch light on, but this was the projects nobody left there light on. I eased in the house and knew Mario had been there because I saw his roaches in the ashtray. I decided

not to turn on the light, I stayed here for three years

so I knew my way around. I sat my keys down by

the door along with my taser as I walked up the hall.

When I opened the door to my bedroom Gee was

sitting on my bed lighting another blunt. I spun

around and tried to run back up the hall way. I

wasn't fast enough because he grabbed me and

covered my mouth.

"If you scream one time you dead, try me!"

I bite down on one of his fingers which

caused him to let me go. I tried to run again but was

tripped by his foot and hit my face on the hard

concrete floor.

"Gavon please stop," I said through my

bloody mouth. My two front teeth were now laying

on the floor.

"Oh you begging now? When I asked you to leave me alone you didn't," he bent down and burned my lip with the blunt. "See a woman like you Chardonnay make men like me snap. My grandma was all I had. Me and you were through so what made you come down to my house that day? HUH?! Because you wanted to be bad and my grandma gone," he started tying me to the bed. He ripped my shirt off and his eye almost bulged out of his head.

"Chardonnay you playing a lot of games. Does your man know you faking this pregnancy? You a snake and you know what we do with snakes?"

He stuffed my mouth with some socks and placed some tape over it. His phone buzzed and he stepped outside the room to answer it.

"Hello? Yea baby, I'm okay. I'll call you when I get home. Ok, love you too."

I knew from the conversation he was talking to Ms. Piggy. I was in a vulnerable state but I was still jealous. I didn't want him but I didn't want anyone else with him either. He pulled the chair that I had in the corner to my bed. He sat there and stared at me with this devilish look in his eyes.

"What's stopping me from killing you? I gave you everything you could ask for but you decided to set me up and try to kill me! When that didn't work you killed my grandma instead!"

His phone buzzed again but he hit the ignore button this time. He pulled a razor blade out of his pocket and got out of the chair. I closed my eyes tight and prepared for the worse.

Chasiti

I was racing through traffic to get to Chardonnay house. I knew he didn't sound like himself. I had followed Gavon the past several days because he had become distant. Not distant as in not being around me but his mind was somewhere else. One day he sat in front of Chardonnay's apartment for twelve hours. He didn't eat or sleep he just stared at her door. I yanked my car in the empty spot and ran as fast as I could to her door. *Jesus please don't let it be locked.* I turned the doorknob and it was unlocked. I didn't want to scare either of them so I walked in slowly. It was dark but there was a dim light at the end of the hall which I believed was her room. I slowly walked down the hall. I could hear Gavon talking to her, his voice was hoarse so I knew he'd been crying.

"Gavon," I said softly. He was straddled over Chardonnay with the blade to her throat.

"Chasiti get out of here!!!," he yelled.

"Gavon," I slowly walked closer to the bed and noticed he was crying. Chardonnay started squirming and trying to say something. The closer I got to Gavon the more I prayed.

"Come here Gavon," I held my hand out for him to get off of Chardonnay. I looked over at Chardonnay rolling her eyes at me. Here I was trying to help her and she was still vindictive.

"Chasiti baby please leave!"

"Come on baby at least give me the blade, Mama Jean wouldn't want this. You have so much to live for and Chardonnay is not worth you losing your life behind bars. What about us?"

I moved as he got off of Chardonnay. He didn't want to give me the blade so I didn't push it. I grabbed his other hand and rubbed it. I looked in his wet eyes, they were red but I knew it wasn't from just crying. Gavon was smoking blunt after blunt. I got down on my knees right in front of Chardonnay.

"Gavon let's pray," I looked up at him. He started pacing in the floor. I already knew his thoughts, he thought he was too far gone for God to forgive him. I wasn't about to let satan win this battle. I bowed my head and started praying out loud.

"Father God, we need you right now. Chardonnay, Gavon and I need you. I'm asking that you forgive Gavon for his actions he took tonight and let him know that it's not too late. And forgive Chardonnay for all her sins, and I ask that after tonight that she begins to experience you. God you know my voice and I ask these things in your son Jesus name Amen."

I looked up to see Gavon on his knees with his face to the ground crying out. I got up to untie Chardonnay. When I looked at her she was crying, I removed the tape from her mouth and pulled the socks out of her mouth. I noticed she was missing two of her teeth that was minor compared to Gavon taking her life.

"Thank you," she said while I untied her feet.

"You're welcome," I smiled at her. I didn't have any beef with her, she hated me from the first time she laid eyes on me.

"Chardonnay can you forgive me?" Gavon was up off the floor and standing over us.

There was a silence that hit the room as we all sat there looking at each other.

"Could you forgive me?" Chardonnay asked.

I knew that was gone be hard for him. I was looking at him waiting on his answer.

"Yea. Only thing I ask is that you stay away from me and my family."

"I'm getting out of here, you don't have to ever worry about me again. Besides Mario will only come and finish what you didn't do."

It was then that I noticed she was no longer pregnant. This girl was way in over her head, I prayed that wherever she ended up at the she stayed out of trouble. I don't think she had too many more chances before someone found her dead.

"Chasiti I'm sorry as well. I had no reason to dislike you, if it wasn't for you I would be dead. And thank you for praying for me. I really needed that."

"So we not gone mention anything that happened here?" Gavon asked.

"Gee I deserve that and so much more. I'm not normal and I know that, me and you would've never worked. My lips are sealed as long as you don't mention to anyone that you saw me."

———————

I slept in the spare room just to make sure Gavon was okay. I woke up and cooked him breakfast and took it upstairs to him. He was already up and making his bed and fully dressed.

"Chas what would I do without you? Here I am trying to get my father out of jail and about to go in. I just snapped, I wasn't thinking at all."

"I don't know what you would do without me, I'm glad I've been watching you just like you been watching Chardonnay. Last night could've been your fate."

"Do you think God will forgive me?"

"He has already forgiven you Gavon, that experience you had at Chardonnay's house was Him."

"What about you? Can you forgive me? Better yet can you trust me?"

"Boy please I know you. And that was not Gavon last night. That was Gee and I believe Gee died last night," I smiled at him.

"Yea he gone," he kissed.

Mario

While Gee was sitting on Chardonnay, I was sitting on both of them. I leaned back in my seat as I watched Chardonnay pack her car with her now empty stomach. I knew she was lying when she wouldn't let me come back in the room with her. Once I did my little investigating I found out she was friends with two of the nurses up there, so while I'm in the waiting area she sitting in one of the rooms talking about the latest fashions.

"Not yet son," my father reached over. I released my grip on the gun. I wanted to off her on the spot but my father was a little more leveled headed than I was. I could stand to learn a few things from him. He's been a free man for twenty years while Gavon daddy sat in jail for the murder my father committed.

"You can't react on impulse. Take your time when you plan to take someone out. We don't know who's watching. We got bigger fish to fry. Word around town is they opening Alvin case back up. If they use Danielle's DNA I'm done. I raped her before I shot her in the head, she always denied me. She was head over hills in love with Alvin, but she couldn't leave the street life alone. So when Reno and Danny wouldn't let me in on their pill and credit card scheme, I decided to take what was most important to them."

Listening to my dad tell me how grimy he was back in the day, made me not trust him. What kind of man would rape a woman and then shoot her in the head. I looked over at him sideways as he smiled. If I didn't know any better, he was in love with Gavon's mother. As soon as I get him out of my car we were done. When my daddy told me Reno and Danny was Gavon uncle's I was done with this whole situation. Those cats was known from bodying people and writing their name on the wall with blood. Who's to say they weren't watching us right now. I never knew Gavon was connected to them, it was truly a small world. Little dude wasn't bout this life, but sometimes you got to give respect where it's due. He didn't have to live the life because he's family name spoke volumes in the streets.

I decided to drop my dad off and just go chill. I was still feeling Chasiti but Gavon won the girl. I didn't deserve her anyway, she couldn't do nothing with a dude like me. I put my car in park and got out hitting the alarm on my Benz.

"Aye young thug, where yo daddy?"

"I just took him home," I said to Reno. Now my daddy bought the drama to my house. I wasn't expecting anyone to know where I laid my head.

"Address?" Danny said.

I couldn't give up my daddy address like that. There was no way in the world, I was gone just let them take my daddy out like that. They felt my resistance Danny grabbed me.

"Aye open the trunk. He don't want to talk so we'll drive around until he ready to talk. We didn't come to kill you young thug. We want yo pappy because he pulled the trigger on our sister." Danny stuffed me in the trunk and snatched my cell phone. The only little bit of hope I had was now in Danny's hands. I didn't believe in God but I hoped they didn't text my daddy like it was me.

The car rode around for a minute, I was starting to become sick from the fumes coming from the exhaust. We came to a stop, and I was wishing on a star we wasn't in front of my daddy house. I heard both car doors slam and I knew from the dogs barking we was at his house. Sometime passed before the trunk popped open and they threw my bleeding father in the trunk with me.

"Daddy...daddy," I tried shaking him.

He opened his eye as much as he could. They beat him pretty badly, my question now was where they were taking us. I had to use the bathroom from being nervous.

"Son, it's over for us. If you believe in a higher power pray. Because we will never see the break of day again."

Before I could respond, I smelled gas and I could hear flames. The car started getting really hot. I didn't know anything about a higher power. I was a G and I was going out like a G looking my father square in the eyes. The streets raised me.

Chasiti

"What would I do without you?" Gavon asked me. We were sitting in my living room watching TV as I retwisted his dreads. I stopped what I was doing to look down into his face. He was so handsome to me. We had endured some of the roughest times in these few months of us being around each other and I wasn't sure that we would make it. We hadn't made things official and some days I thought that God was trying to pull us a part.

But now as I sat and looked at him I knew that was only the enemy that was trying to sow that seed of discord but God had still prevailed.

I didn't have an answer for him and I don't think that he really needed one from me. The smile I had on my face was enough for him to know I understood what he was feeling because I was feeling the same way. After that horrible relationship I had previously I had almost given up on love but somehow it had found me again and the feeling was euphoric. Instead of answering him I bent down to give him a kiss that explained my feelings better than any word that left my lips could. God knows I had to get myself under control because my flesh was acting up at the moment.

"Jesus keep me near the cross." I said breathing heavily. This man just did something to me and I knew that if we ever got to that intimate place it would be like nothing either of us had experienced before. I was still a virgin and I knew that he wasn't, but I knew that if God united us it would blow the both of our minds. Because our relationship with each other and with God had a chance to grow before sex clouded our minds, I knew that if and when we did I was never coming down from that high.

I hadn't realized I had my eyes closed for so long. I was just enjoying the moment but when I did open them I got the shock of my life. Gavon was on one knee holding a little velvet box. I couldn't stop the tears if I wanted to as he began to speak.

"Chasiti I don't know where I would be right now if you didn't come into my life when you did. I know I had been knowing you since we were younger but not on this level. I now understand what it means to have God present to me my good thing. You are my good thing Chas. Through you and Mama Jean I understand just how much God really loves me.

I never desired to be married because all I was around were women who constantly threw themselves at me and it was too easy to get them. That's not what I wanted in a wife so I was content with what I was doing. Then here you come with standards and morals that made me want to take a deeper look and without me knowing I fell hard for you. Not to mention you saved your boy's life," he chuckled.

I was so at a loss for words because of what he was expressing to me.

"You didn't only save my life physically by giving me blood, you saved my life spiritually. If it wasn't for you I would be dead in more ways than one. Mama Jean said that you were to be my wife and I thought she was just saying something until the other night when you stopped me from killing Chardonnay and how you showed forgiveness even after all that she has put you through. Chas I love you and I guess I said all of that just to ask will you marry me? I don't want anybody but you and I'm finally ready to settle down and start a family," he ended.

"Yes baby I'll marry you. Oh my God yes!" I said excitedly. God had finally answered my prayers. I was about to become Mrs. Gavon Maurice Cunningham.

I looked at the ring that he placed on my finger and it was gorgeous. I guess the look I had on my face caused him to explain how he got it.

"I didn't steal it." He said and it caused me to laugh.

"I know that boy," I said slapping him on his arm. But I was curious as to how he paid for this ring that looked to be about a carat and a half.

"With everything going on I never did get to show you this." He said getting up and going into the kitchen. I heard him open and close one of the drawers and he soon came into view again holding two envelopes. One was thin and the other was a thick manila one. He sat down beside me and handed me the thinner one first.

"What's this?" I asked him as I held it. I knew it as something that had to be good by the big grin he had on his face.

"Baby just open it." He was getting impatient so I turned it over to read the front. I looked up at him because it was addressed to him from his mother.

I quickly opened it as I read aloud,

To my Al and baby boy Gavon,

If the two of you are reading this without me then I know that I am no longer here with you any longer. My street life has finally called me home. I apologize for the pain and suffering that my selfish decisions has caused you. It's something about when you get so far into this life that it's hard to get out of. It's only two ways and we know what those are.

Al thank you so much for loving me flaws and all. I saw what you were trying to do by working hard and being a provider and no matter how bad you wanted me to let the streets go, the streets wouldn't let me go. Everything that you did for me and our son was straight from the heart and I love you more than anything. Please don't hate me for not listening. You know how stubborn I was. Mama always tried telling me and my brother's about God and how He loved us and would forgive us. I guess just like so many others we tell ourselves that we have to fix ourselves before we come to God and that couldn't be further from the truth. It's because we can't fix our lives and that's what He sent His son for.

Mama didn't know this, well no one knew, but I have given my life over to God and asked Jesus to come into my heart. My plan is to let you know on our anniversary that's coming up but just in case I'm not here there is no question in your minds about how my soul left.

Gavon my baby boy. God knew the moment I looked into your eyes when you were born I fell so

*in love with you. All I could think about was how I
had been blessed to have you in my life. You were
conceived with so much love between your father
and I. Please don't take the path that my brother's
and I took early in life. I could look at you and tell
that this life wasn't in you and I want nothing more
than for you to grow up to be an outstanding man
like your father.*

*I knew that at any moment I could be gone.
So I opened up an account in Gavon's name with
every dime I had. I don't want to risk having anyone
coming to where I lay my head with my family and
harm you because I have something stashed there.
Like the good book says, 'The wealth of the wicked
shall be stored up for the righteous. Didn't think I
knew that huh? Lol*

*Anyway use this money to take care of the
two of you and Mama. I'm giving this letter to my*

brother's to keep because they will know the right

time to give it to you. I love the both of you so much

and I pray that one day we get to see each other

again.

Love Danielle/Mommy

I was such a crybaby as I finished reading what Gavon's mother had written. My soul cried out full of joy that she had been saved before she had been killed. She was one of the few that took heed to the voice of God when it was time to turn her life over to Him and I'm so happy that she did.

There was still something else in the envelope so I took it out to see what it was and what I saw had blown me away. It was a bank statement showing a balance of close to five and a half million dollars. Because the type of account she had it in the money just kept growing over time.

"God never ceases to amaze me. Do you see this Gavon?" I asked him.

"Yea that's a lot of money and she made sure that my dad and I would be taken care of."

"No not just that but the amount is even spiritual," I informed him. I could tell by the look on his face he was clueless to what I meant so I explained. "The number five symbolizes God's grace, goodness, and favor. Five multiplied by itself is twenty five which means grace upon grace. Hence the five point five million."

The look on his face told me that this still wasn't making sense to him but the more he got into his word and studied then it would one day. Until then I would just continue to help him.

"This was how I was able to help open my Dad's case back up. I split it in half and opened him his own account for when he comes home and then I used part of what I had left to get this." He said handing me the thicker envelope.

If I hadn't been sitting down then I probably would have been hitting the floor at that exact moment. I was holding in my hand the deed to a four bedroom, three bath home that had both Gavon's and my name on it. He had paid attention to me when I told him that I hated houses with garages. Why I didn't know but that stuck out to me as well. I had always been taught that the number 430 represented the fulfillment of the promises of God. Four bedrooms, three baths, no garage. Mama Jean had said so many times that God promised her that He wouldn't let Gavon fall victim to the streets, and once again that promise had been kept.

"When can we go see it?" I asked jumping up excited.

"Let's go shawty." He said.

Just as we were about to head out of the door we heard a breaking news report come on the tv that caught the both of our attention.

"I'm here in Port Wentworth where a vehicle was found by one of the sugar refinery's employees burning about half a mile from the plant. Witness stated that he was just getting off of his shift and heading home when he saw the car beginning to go up in flames. Although the fire seemed to have been just set a few minutes before, whoever the suspect was had left undetected.

Police have not released an official statement but there were two bodies found in the trunk of the 1989 Crown Victoria. Anyone with information on this crime can call our Crime stoppers tip line at 912-234-2020. I'm Tonya

Reynolds for WSATV Live. Back to you Ashley and Steve."

Gavon turned to me but no words needed to be said between the two of us. I could tell we were both thinking the same thing, that his uncles were involved but neither of us wanted to address it. I hated for anyone to lose their lives but there is always a time where we must reap what we sow. I knew the bodies found were the ones of Mario and his father but it was nothing that we could do about it now but pray that justice was served.

EPILOGE

Gavon

"Forgiveness isn't for the person that wronged you. Forgiveness is for you. There is no way that we can enter the Kingdom of heaven or expect for God to forgive our faults if we can't do the same for others. Isn't that the whole idea of serving God and being Christlike in the first place? If I hadn't forgiven some people then I wouldn't be where I am today. It's time to let it go. The doors of the church are open." I said as I watched the people slowly line up in front of the altar.

There were about ten people standing there and I was glad that they had chosen to come before God but there was one in particular that stood out. I looked over at my wife as she smiled and walked down from where she was previously sitting. One of the ushers had to help her because her pregnant belly hid the steps beneath her. Chasiti was eight months pregnant with our daughter Danielle Jean and I could tell that she was ready to come out.

I watched as she went over to the woman with tears in her eyes as she held her arms out for a hug. Instantly Chardonnay welcomed her embrace as they cried together. The last time we had seen her was the night I almost took her life. From the looks of it she was doing ok. She looked genuinely happy and my heart was filled with joy for her. She too had received a new life from the Lord and I prayed that she stayed on that path. Just like me she had a story to tell that could reach so many for the kingdom and I hoped she used it for the good of others.

My father was standing behind me with a look of pride on his face as he put his hand on my shoulder. Because of the witness who found the car burning with the bodies of Mario and his father in it had called in time to salvage the bodies. Once they ran the DNA they found out that the sample taken from my mother matched the one from Mario's father. All of this time he was thinking that my mother had money in the house but she had been smart not to. When he didn't find any and she wouldn't tell him where it was he killed her right before my father walked in the door. It had taken twenty three years to get the truth but I had gotten my father back and my mother was resting in peace finally. The relationship that we had was unbreakable and I was thankful to God for that.

My uncles were still out in the streets heavy but they had already made up in their minds long ago that living right wasn't for them. So I just keep them in prayer and see them every once in a while. No one ever came forward with any information about the murders but we all knew who had their hands in that. I was just glad that I didn't have that lingering over my head.

Chasiti and I couldn't have been happier. The love I had for her ran so deep and I was blessed to have her by my side. Now she was the true definition of a rider and she stood by me through it all. Here we were about to be parents in a few weeks and I couldn't ask for anything more. The more she prayed with me and I got closer to God I finally understood what my calling was. I would have never in a million years thought I would become a pastor but God showed me that the life I used to live was only for me to be able to bring about change in other men and women who struggled with the same issues. He had turned my test into a testimony. I was on my way to heaven, so there was no more Thuggin at the Altar for me.

Their End....Your Beginning...

Sometimes with the life we live it's hard to not let the world suck us in. Daily we fall short but daily we can also submit to God. If you haven't received the gift of salvation or have been backsliding this is your time. No matter where you are right now you can surrender to Him. Let Him guide you in the way that He wants you to go. It doesn't take a lot to just confess your sins and accept Jesus in.

If you are one of the ones that God is speaking to right now don't let this moment pass you by. He doesn't expect you to have your life together, that's what He's here for.

Say, Lord Jesus I believe you died on the cross and I believe that You rose again. I know that I have not been faithful in the ways that you have wanted me to go so I ask that right now that you forgive me of my sins. Not just the ones that are known but even the ones that are unknown and may seem insignificant. I trust you and no matter how I feel I know that you have received me in. Thank you Lord for loving me. In your Son Jesus' name, Amen.

CPSIA information can be obtained at www.ICGtesting.com
Printed in the USA
LVOW10s1517060516

487047LV00017B/647/P